TRAPPED IN THE MINE!

"Let's go down!" cried Nelson.

"Are you sure the ladder will hold us?" asked Ted, a little more cautiously.

Nelson hauled up the rope ladder and tested its rungs.

"It'll hold an elephant. Come on!"

Suiting his actions to his words, Nelson grabbed the flashlight and began the descent, soon standing at the bottom of the shaft and calling impatiently for his companion to follow. Ted was lighter than Nelson, who was inclined to be overweight, so it is not easy to understand what followed. Apparently the rope hanging on one of the nails had slipped farther toward the head of the nail, thus creating added pressure downward.

Ted had barely begun the descent when the nail bent slightly. There was a splintering of the wood, which must have been weakened by exposure and dampness, and the nail gave way altogether. The sudden doubling of weight on the other nail also caused it to bend, and the rope ladder fell off entirely, dropping Ted to the bottom of the shaft with a suppressed cry.

Had the ladder fallen from both nails at the same instant he might have escaped injury, but because one nail gave way first he dropped at an angle, and his ankle crumbled beneath him. He lay where he fell, stunned, unable to rise to his feet.

THE TED WILFORD SERIES

1. *The Secret of Thunder Mountain* (1951)
2. *The Locked Safe Mystery* (1954)
3. *The Star Reporter Mystery* (1955)
4. *The Singing Trees Mystery* (1956)
5. *The Empty House Mystery* (1957)
6. *The Counterfeit Mystery* (1958)
7. *The Stolen Plans Mystery* (1959)
8. *The Scarecrow Mystery* (1960)
9. *The Big Cat Mystery* (1961)
10. *The Missing Witness Mystery* (1962)
11. *The Baseball Mystery* (1963)
12. *The Mystery of Rainbow Gulch* (1964)
13. *The Abandoned Mine Mystery* (1965)
14. *The S. S. Shamrock Mystery* (1966)
15. *The Greenhouse Mystery* (1967)

THE SECRET OF THUNDER MOUNTAIN

TED WILFORD MYSTERY SERIES

NORVIN PALLAS

WILDSIDE PRESS

ACKNOWLEDGMENTS

The Wildside Press reprints of the Ted Wilford series were made possible by the assistance of many people, including Norvin Pallas's family; Steve Romberger, whose copy of *The Secret of Thunder Mountain* was ultimately used to create this edition; George Beatty and James D. Keeline, who provided copies of many of the texts and covers; and David M. Baumann, whose essay "A Dark Horse Series" was an invaluable reference for reprinting the stories; and of course Wildside's production team, Shawn Garrett, Helen McGee, and Sam Hogan.

Published by Wildside Press LLC.
www.wildsidepress.com

CHAPTER 1

Old Goldie's Mine

The next North Ridge batter was a heavy hitter. Ted Wilford knew it, and instinctively moved back fifteen paces, playing a deep center field. With one out in the first half of the ninth inning, and two runners on base, North Ridge was threatening the narrow two-run lead which the Forestdale team had managed to build up through eight innings of spirited attack and steady defense. The North Ridge captain, his face a study in determination, came forward swinging two bats. One of them he tossed back toward the bench, then took his place at the left side of the plate.

Nelson Morgan, crouched behind the plate, studied the batter's stance carefully, then called for a fast ball low and outside. The ball came true, straight toward Nelson's glove, and the batter took a wicked cut at it. Although swinging a little late, he met it squarely, and the ball rose in a high arc far above the heads of the infielders and out between left and center fields.

At the crack of the bat Ted turned and dashed out with his back to the plate, cutting toward left field and running at full speed. Over his shoulder he saw the ball descending upon him, and at the last instant, still running full tilt, he stretched out his arms as far as he could reach, and managed to grasp the ball with the tip of his glove. He stumbled a little, but hung on to ball. The runner on third scored easily after the catch, but had Ted missed the ball it would probably have fallen for a home run. As it was, the next batter drove a hard grounder down third base, and was thrown out at first, ending the game with a score of three to two in favor of Forestdale. Ted trotted in off the field, the applause of the spectators still ringing pleasantly in his ears.

"Nice catch!" called Nelson, patting him on the back. "Any time we can beat North Ridge two years in a row, we must be good or lucky."

"Or both," suggested Ted with a grin.

"Coming?" asked Nelson, as Ted made no move to follow him.

"In a minute."

"Oh, sure," returned Nelson with a knowing smile, catching sight of Margaret Lake sitting in the first row of the stands. He turned and trotted toward the school building. Ted walked over to the stands where Margaret was gathering her notes together. Most of the spectators were leaving the field. A few voices called out to him, and he waved his hand in recognition.

"Ted, you were wonderful!" Margaret greeted him. "Just wait till I write the story for the *Statesman*. You'll be a real hero."

"Margaret, you wouldn't dare!" gasped Ted in dismay.

"All right, Ted, I'll tone my story down, just for you." She turned toward a small boy, about eight years old, sitting next to her. "Ted, I want you to meet Tim, a friend of mine." Ted had not realized before that the boy was with Margaret. Tim was neatly but inexpensively dressed in a white sports shirt with a sprawling monogram on the pocket, short brown cloth trousers, socks, and sandals. Since Forestdale was only a small town, Ted knew that Tim must be an out-of-town visitor.

"How do you do?" said Ted gravely, extending his hand, quite as though he were being introduced to an adult.

"Hello," said Tim, accepting Ted's hand. He added shyly, "I wish I could play center field like that."

"Some day you can," said Ted easily, and then bit his lip sharply. He had not noticed before that the boy was crippled.

His right leg was noticeably deformed, and later when he walked it seemed as though it might collapse altogether beneath him.

"It was a good game," said Tim happily, "and may a bolt of lightning strike me down if it wasn't." Ted and Margaret exchanged smiles. Where had the boy picked up such a curious expression? They were almost the last to leave the stands and cross the field toward the school. Tim's progress was very slow and difficult, and Ted longed to pick him up and carry him over his shoulder. But not wishing to embarrass the boy, he satisfied himself by grasping the small hand tightly.

"Did you notice what our newspaper assignment was this week?" asked Margaret.

"Yes, an interview with some prominent person. Have you chosen anyone?"

"Miss Benhardt is in town," returned Margaret. Ted did not recognize the name immediately. "She used to be a singer on the network. That ought to make a good story."

Ted nodded in agreement. "How about you, Ted?"

Ted said slowly, "I don't know. I was thinking about trying to get an interview with Old Goldie."

She opened her brown eyes wide in surprise. "With Old Goldie!" she repeated.

"Yes," said Ted, with decision. "It would be a good story, if I can get it."

"If you can get it," Margaret agreed skeptically. They had reached the building, and Ted left them, after acknowledging his introduction to Tim by ruffling his hair in a friendly manner. He entered the school and went downstairs. The locker room had about cleared out, except for Nelson, who was waiting, and another group of players just leaving.

"Nice catch, Wilford," called one of them.

"What did you do, fly after it?" asked another in amusement.

"Shucks, I didn't do anything, let me alone," said Ted. They went out laughing, leaving Ted in confusion. Nelson did not refer to the game. He waited until Ted returned from the shower room, then sat near him, placing one foot on the bench and coupling his hands about his knee.

"It took you long enough," he complained.

"Yes. Margaret had a little crippled boy with her."

"I know, I saw him before. Is he her cousin?"

"She didn't say." Ted combed back his hair. "Nelson, what do you think about Old Goldie's mine?"

"Think about it!" exclaimed Nelson. "I wish I had it. I'd buy a yacht, and build a private swimming pool, and have a gallon of ice cream a day."

"No, you wouldn't," contradicted Ted. "You'd put aside money for college first thing, just like I would. I've been wondering, though, do you think Old Goldie really has a secret gold mine somewhere on Thunder Mountain?"

"I don't know," said Nelson thoughtfully. "Ever since I was real little I can remember old timers looking up at the mountains and saying, 'There's gold in the hills.' But nobody ever found any gold."

"Unless Old Goldie did. Remember years ago when all those stories were going around about his mine?"

"I remember, but in spite of all the rumors nobody was ever able to prove that Old Goldie had a gold mine. How did those stories get started anyway?"

"I was talking to Ronald about that the other day," Ted proceeded. "The way it was supposed to have happened, Old Goldie was in North Ridge, purchasing his supplies for a few months ahead. He didn't have enough money to meet his bill, so he offered a gold nugget in payment! How that grocery clerk's eyes must have popped out! The story was all over North Ridge by evening, and all over the county, I guess, in a week. Everybody just dropped whatever he was doing and headed for the hills."

"And everybody came back empty-handed," finished Nelson. "This is all very interesting, but I don't know how we began talking about Old Goldie."

"It's our newspaper assignment this week," explained Ted, stepping into his regular shoes, and putting each foot on the bench in turn to tie the laces. "We need to interview someone, and I thought I'd tackle Old Goldie."

Nelson whistled. "You like to make things hard for yourself, don't you? Why, nobody knows anything about Old Goldie, his real name or where he came from or even where he is most of the time."

"That's why it ought to make a good story," defended Ted.

"Sure, and just how are you going to get it?"

"Well, first thing, I thought I'd ask Ron about it. He might know what to do."

"You think your brother Ronald knows everything."

"No, but he usually has a pretty good idea where he can find out anything he wants to know." He stepped in front of the mirror to knot his tie. "Say, I'm not keeping you too long, am I?"

"Oh, don't mind about me. We're probably locked in the building, and we'll starve to death, and Monday morning they'll find us lying there—"

Ted brought this tirade to an end with the effective use of a wet towel. Shortly afterward, they left the building. At Settler's Elm, where the huge tree divides Main Street, they separated, and Ted turned in at the office of the *Town Crier*, to find Ronald waiting for him.

"I see that you won," observed Ronald, accepting the lifting of the corners of Ted's mouth as a barometer. "Was it a tight game?"

"Swell. They threatened right up to the end, but we held them."

"And how did you do?" asked Ronald, with elder brother curiosity.

"Got a double out of five, and caught four flies," replied Ted, quickly passing over the importance of his defensive play.

"I wish I could have seen the game, but I only got in fifteen minutes ago." Ronald sat back in the large swivel chair. "Now what's on your mind?"

"Ron, I want to get an interview with Old Goldie for our school newspaper." Ronald's reaction was the same as Nelson's; he, too, whistled. "That's going to be tough. I suppose if you do find him, you think he'll tell you all about his mine, and everything else you want to know."

"Well, no, but even if he acted mysterious, that would still make a good story, wouldn't it?"

"You may have something there, Ted," said Ronald, quick to notice Ted's slight disappointment. "The problem, then, is to find Old Goldie.

He gets his supplies in either Forestdale or North Ridge. He hasn't been seen around here, so our point of attack is North Ridge." He reached for the telephone.

"Are you calling Ken Kutler?"

"Mr. Kenneth Kutler would as soon part with a tooth as with a story." Ronald laughed. "No, I have another secret source. The chief constable sometimes tips me off on stories, and that's how I've managed to get some scoops right out from under Ken's nose. I once did a favor for Constable Mulgrew that he considered pretty important." From the telephone conversation that followed, Ted could grasp very little, but when Ronald turned away his face was serious.

"I'm sorry, Ted, but Old Goldie died today in the North Ridge hospital."

CHAPTER 2

The Envelope

It is a shock to learn of the passing of someone you have known. Old Goldie had seemed so much a part of the town, like Thunder Mountain and Roaring River, something that had always been there and always will be there. And years later, when hiking along the river banks, you may glance up suddenly and half expect to see his gray-haired, slightly stooped figure. Ted felt his eyes growing tight.

"I suppose that's the end of my newspaper story," he said soberly.

"Yes, that ends your chance for an interview," Ronald agreed, "but it's beginning to look as though it's now my story instead of yours. Constable Mulgrew told me how it happened. Old Goldie must have been returning from some long expedition to the northwest when he was taken ill on the road. A passing motorist picked him up and drove him into North Ridge, but by that time he had become much worse. Constable Mulgrew went through his effects afterward, and he told me what he found."

Suddenly Ted perked to attention. "You mean they found something that told who he was?"

"No, not exactly. There wasn't much to help—only some clothes, a little money, a few rock samples, a wedding ring—"

"A wedding ring!" echoed Ted. "Do you suppose Old Goldie was married at some time, and maybe it didn't turn out so well, and that's how he became a prospector?"

"It's a good story," Ronald smiled, "but it doesn't quite fit the facts. There was an inscription inside the ring, most of it worn off, but they could make out the letters MASS and the date June 17, 1873. It was apparently his mother's wedding ring."

"Then he wasn't married—he didn't have anyone. It makes it seem worse, doesn't it, that he was all alone, no friends or relatives. I don't suppose we'll ever know who he was now."

"Well, there was one other thing—an envelope with a picture in it. Constable Mulgrew thinks that might be a clue, so I'm running over to North Ridge tonight."

"May I come, too?" asked Ted eagerly.

"Mm, no, Ted, I don't think so, not this time. We planned on going to the movies tonight with Mother, and I don't think we should both run out. Anyway, this is quite a confidential matter, and Mulgrew mightn't be quite so willing to talk with you there. I'll tell you all about it when I get back."

Walking over to the file, Ronald pulled out a drawer and began to rummage through the folders. The *Town Crier* was a semi-weekly paper, coming out on Tuesdays and Fridays. It attempted to cover only the local news, since most of its readers subscribed to one of the big dailies as well. At last Ronald found the folder he wanted and brought it back to the desk.

"This doesn't look as though it will help us very much. These old clippings merely tell that Old Goldie had been in town again. It's been that way for fifteen years. Up until six or seven years ago he was usually seen with Jim Rivers, the Indian guide. But since that time nothing more has been seen of Jim."

"I remember Jim," Ted recalled. "He was the only Indian I'd ever seen. I guess I was kind of afraid of him when I was small."

"I was hoping there was a picture in here," said Ronald, returning the folder to the file. "I'm sure I saw a picture of Old Goldie not so very long ago, and so far as I know it's the only one in existence."

"In Nelson's album," said Ted promptly. "He snapped it down by the river last summer, and he brought the set over when he had it finished."

"That's right." Ronald clicked his tongue. "Say, Ted, you could do something for me. I wish you'd get a copy of that picture and bring it down to the office tomorrow. We'll pay for it, of course."

"Sure thing," Ted agreed.

"Don't tell Nelson any more than you have to," Ronald cautioned. "I can't hope to keep the story of Old Goldie's death from spreading, but I'd like to cover up these other little details until next Tuesday." Ronald turned off the lights and locked the door behind them as they left the office. As they passed near the school, music came faintly to their ears.

"The band practicing so late?" asked Ronald.

"Yes, drilling for the Memorial Day parade next week. It's been a long time since the football season, and they get rusty over the winter. Shall we watch them for a while?"

It was not yet six o'clock, and Ronald was agreeable. Somehow the music reminded both of them of the coming summer. They stood near the fence as the drum major directed the band through an intricate countermarch. Then with high steps and twirling baton he led them proudly down the field. The whistle blew, the baton stood poised, the drums finished the cadence, gave the quick beats of the roll off, and the band broke into the strains of the Marine Hymn.

When the last notes had died away, the drum major dismissed the members, some of them running wildly across the field while the others followed more leisurely. Those who passed close by waved at Ted, and someone shouted congratulations on the catch he had made.

"What was that?" asked Ronald, pricking up his ears.

"Oh, it wasn't anything," said Ted with reluctance. "I'll tell you about it when we get home."

* * * *

They turned away from the field and arrived home on the hour, their appetites eager to do full justice to their mother's excellent cooking. Ted related the full story of the baseball game, making as light of his own part as possible, while Ronald mentioned Old Goldie's death, and that he felt obliged to run over to North Ridge that evening.

"If Ted wants to go with you," said Mrs. Wilford, "we can go to the movies some other night."

"No, Mom, I'm afraid Ted would only have to spend most of the evening waiting in the car. I'd better leave now. I don't know when I'll be back, but I'll try not to be any later than I can help." He gave his mother a kiss. Ted went out with him to the garage, and opened the doors.

It was always a surprise to both brothers when Jeremiah, Ronald's ancient car, started on the first trial, but this time it did, and Ronald waved his arm in a Victory salute to Ted in parting. Ronald Wilford could easily lay claim to being the star reporter for the *Town Crier*, chiefly because he was the only person serving in that capacity. The editor, Mr. Christopher Dobson, affectionately known as Crusty, and the secretary, Miss Monroe, completed the front-office staff, while the printer and his assistant occupied the larger room in the rear.

Nevertheless, Ronald took his position quite as seriously as though he were working on a large metropolitan daily. When he felt he had done a good job, he experienced a glow of satisfaction, and when Kenneth Kutler of the North Ridge News Record beat him out on a story, he became, as Ted said, so dumpy that you could hardly speak to him for the rest of the day.

Stopping at the North Ridge police station, Ronald learned that Constable Mulgrew had left for home. He drove on to the constable's residence, where the officer and his wife greeted him warmly.

"I suppose this is what you came about," said Mulgrew, drawing an envelope from his inside coat pocket and handing it to Ronald. The envelope was dirty and ragged at the edges, as if it had been carried in someone's pocket for a long time. Printed with pencil in large block letters were the initials T.A.F. Ronald looked up inquiringly.

"Is there anything to indicate these might be Old Goldie's initials?"

"No, it doesn't seem probable. You might put your initials on an article, so that in case you mislaid it, it could be returned to you, but if no one knew your initials anyway, what would be the use? No, this looks as though the initials belong to the person the envelope was intended for."

"But you have no idea who that person is?"

"None whatever. When you look inside, I think you're going to get a surprise."

Opening the envelope, Ronald took out a small snapshot. It was a picture of a log cabin, in front of which stood three pine trees. But the most startling feature was that on one of the trees was a large, white letter X. He controlled an impulse to whistle; the constable grinned.

"Makes you start thinking, doesn't it?"

"It'll make a lot of people start thinking," Ronald returned. "Does Ken Kutler know anything about this envelope?"

"Not yet."

"Is there any reason that he has to?"

"I'll tell you, I've got an awfully poor memory sometimes. But I can't ever forget, last summer when my wife needed a blood transfusion, how you stayed up all night until you located a suitable donor. I've got an idea I'm going to forget to mention this envelope to Kutler for a few days."

"Thanks. Would it be possible for me to have this photograph copied?"

"I think so. Get it back to me by noon tomorrow, and it'll be all right."

Thanking him again, and expressing his best wishes to Mrs. Mulgrew, Ronald left a few minutes later. He stopped at the hospital to talk to a member of the staff. Then, back at the *Town Crier*, he busied himself for another hour searching through the files. When he arrived home, Ted was already asleep.

Early Saturday morning, when Ted knocked and was admitted to his brother's room, he found Ronald standing before the mirror, an electric razor buzzing in his hand. Carefully Ronald maneuvered the instrument up and down his cheeks, a completely unnecessary operation, for he had no need to shave beyond the slight bristle on his chin and upper lip.

"What did you find out about the envelope?" asked Ted eagerly.

"Oh, yes, the envelope," said Ronald carelessly, as if he had just remembered it. He surveyed himself in the mirror to make sure that the nonexistent hair had been removed in a manner befitting the chief reporter on the Forestdale *Town Crier*. Satisfied that his face now looked quite as well as nature had intended, he shut off the razor, deposited it in the dresser drawer, and struggled into his tie and coat.

"You'll find the envelope in the top drawer of my desk."

"Ron! He let you take it?"

"Yes, Constable Mulgrew places a high value on friendship."

"And Ken Kutler doesn't know about it—"

"Not yet. He may get on to it. Another officer and a member of the hospital staff know about it, but if Mr. Kutler happens to be a little careless checking details, there's no reason why I ought to call him up and tell him about it, is there?"

But Ted was already busy examining the envelope. "T.A.F.!" he exclaimed. In his mind he tried to recall all the families he knew whose names began with F. Ronald watched him in amusement.

"I've done a little better than you," he said, correctly guessing Ted's chain of thought. "I've checked the telephone directory and also our newspaper file. I don't believe there is anyone in Forestdale with those initials."

Slipping the picture from the envelope, Ted studied it intently. At last he looked up, puzzled.

"Ron, what does this all mean?"

"Well," Ronald considered carefully, "let us suppose that Old Goldie had a friend whose initials were T.A.F., and that he wanted to leave a message for that friend which, for obvious reasons, he didn't care to put into words. What would the message be likely to be about—except to explain the location of his secret gold mine!"

A clue to the lost mine! Ted sat bolt upright.

"Ron!"

"Yes, Ted, this seems to be the only message that Old Goldie left—a picture of a cabin on a hill, three trees in front, an X on one of the trees. I'm afraid this is the only clue we'll ever have to the location of Old Goldie's mine!"

CHAPTER 3

What the Town Thought

"Ron, are we imagining all this?" asked Ted in wonder. "Everybody's been looking for that mine for years, and no one ever found it. Some engineers even made a careful survey, and couldn't find any traces of gold. I guess I've always had a secret hunch that the gold mine was just a story."

Ronald considered. "Well, Ted, this much seems to be true: On several occasions Old Goldie did pay for some of his purchases with small gold nuggets. He must have been getting his gold from some place."

"But he might have been saving those nuggets from way back. If he had a gold mine, why didn't he file a claim to it? Why didn't he work it enough so that he'd be rich, and wouldn't have to live like a tramp?"

"I don't think we'll be able to answer those questions, Ted, until we find out more about Old Goldie. But suppose he did have a mine to which, for some reason, he didn't care to file a claim. Now supposing he had a friend to whom he wanted to leave the mine, he couldn't will the mine to his friend legally, and he certainly wouldn't have cared to carry a message about giving the location of the mine. Then perhaps he would make some arrangement for leaving the message in the form of a picture, which only his friend, T.A.F., would understand."

"But Old Goldie didn't have any friends."

"Oh, come, Ted, how can you say that any person doesn't have a friend? No one knows anything about Old Goldie up until fifteen years ago, so who can say what happened before that?"

"If that's true, Ron, then when you publish the picture this man T.A.F.—it would have to be a man, wouldn't it?— he'll know where the mine is. But if you didn't publish the picture—"

"Sorry, Ted, there's not a chance. I'm a reporter, and I'm working on a story. Otherwise this envelope would never have been given to me. I wouldn't have the right to suppress this picture, even if I could."

Ted looked crestfallen, even though he had known that was what Ronald would say. "Then there's no chance of our discovering the mine first."

"I wouldn't go so far as to say that," cautioned Ronald. "The message might have been meant for someone else, and still tell us a few things. Let's look that picture over."

He sat down on the bed and leaned over Ted's shoulder as they studied the snapshot for some minutes.

"This is undoubtedly Old Goldie's own cabin," Ronald began, "or at least one of his cabins. He wouldn't have entrusted a secret like this to a cabin where someone else was likely to stay. How far away is his cabin? Probably not too far. He purchased his supplies in Forestdale or North Ridge, so it is probably within fairly easy walking distance.

Would his cabin be likely to be very close to his mine? I should be inclined to answer yes. He might as well stay there as anywhere else, and perhaps maintain a kind of guard over it.

"Now where is this cabin? Notice that he purchased his supplies in Forestdale or North Ridge. Apparently it didn't make much difference to him. Now in this picture it is very clear that the cabin is located on a steep hill—"

"Thunder Mountain!" exclaimed Ted. "That's where everybody thought the mine was."

"Yes, Thunder Mountain, or the hills to the north or south. I've checked the distances on a map, and tried to estimate walking distances, and I believe that Thunder Mountain would be just about equally distant from Forestdale and North Ridge."

"Where on Thunder Mountain, Ron? Everybody's searched on Thunder Mountain, and they've never found his cabin."

"Yes, but not having this picture they wouldn't have known whether it was his cabin or not, unless they found him there. However, I would suppose that the cabin is in some out-of-the way place, possibly concealed, but in any case somewhat off from the main trails. Now which side of the mountain is it on?"

"The eastern slope," Ted hazarded. "That's closer to Forestdale."

"Study that picture closely, Ted. It was taken in the bright sunshine, probably during the summer. Notice how distinct the shadows are. Yet the shadow of the cabin is rather short, proving that the picture was taken at about noon. Now notice how all the shadows fall to the left. At noon the shadows always point to the north. In that case the left-hand side of this picture must represent north, the cabin itself must face toward the west, and it must be located on the western slope of the hill or mountain."

Ted's eyes brightened as Ronald explained his theory, and a thrill of excitement crept through him which he kept under control only with difficulty. "Even so, there must be dozens of cabins on the western slope of Thunder Mountain."

"Perhaps we can carry our reasoning one step farther. Is this cabin located high or low?"

"You can't tell," Ted decided. "The picture doesn't show the sky, so maybe that means low."

"I wasn't thinking of the picture. I was thinking about the engineers, testing the streams for traces of gold. They never found any, which suggests to me that the mine must be located some distance away from any stream or fast-running water. I'm not a good enough geologist to know, but I should think this would be more likely to occur at some high point, where the accumulation of water is less, and the surface water runs off in such a fashion that it has less chance to pick up traces of gold."

For the first time Ted looked doubtful and Ronald smiled.

"Well, I don't insist upon it."

"Suppose we did find the cabin, Ron, then what do we do about the tree with the X carved on the bark? Is that where we're supposed to dig?"

"Whoa, Ted, you're going too fast. First, I don't think there is any tree with an X on it. If you look at the picture closely, I think you'll agree there is something a little queer about that X. It's meant to look as though the X were carved there, but I don't think it is. That would be too obvious a clue, wouldn't it, in case someone happened to stumble across the tree. I believe the X is on the picture, not on the tree. If the negative had been touched up in black, that would make any X appear white on the picture. To answer your question, no, I don't think that is the place to dig. I imagine that pine tree is a kind of landmark, about which Mr. T.A.F. already knows, from which he can calculate the location of the mine."

"Whee!" exclaimed Ted, "you've figured things pretty closely." But as he examined each link in the chain of evidence, it seemed to ring true. The light of hope flashed in his eyes, only to be dimmed by a disconcerting thought. "Gosh, Ron, it would take days to go to Thunder Mountain and search the western slope, and there's still two weeks of school left."

Ronald envisioned his own assignments piled up before him. "I know, and I can't very well get away right now, either."

"Jimmy, in two weeks T.A.F. will have found the mine and claimed it, and there won't be anything we can do."

"Don't be too sure, Ted. I don't think Old Goldie wanted to make it too easy for anyone to find his mine. Our T.A.F. may have his difficulties, too. He'll have a two weeks' start, but if he doesn't find the mine by then, you and Nelson will have your chance."

While speaking, he had been gathering together various papers and stuffing them into a brief case. The envelope was placed very carefully into a larger envelope and in his inside coat pocket. The appetizing aroma of frying buckwheat cakes was already noticeable, and the brothers descended the stairs together. Mrs. Wilford would have been an unimaginative woman indeed had she failed to notice Ted's air of suppressed excitement and Ronald's exaggerated nonchalance at breakfast that morning, but although she was interested in the activities of her sons, she was not an inquisitive or prying type of woman. She knew that when her boys were puzzling over a problem, they often preferred to keep their troubles to themselves, but as soon as they had reached a decision, or felt the need of her advice, they would come to her. So she asked no questions, but kept the table conversation on general topics.

"These cakes are dandy," exclaimed Ronald with enthusiasm, as his mother refilled his plate. Finally he pushed back his chair, declaring himself unable to eat another morsel. Ted walked with him as far as the corner, then returned slowly to the house. With the passing of his first feeling of elation, doubts began to creep back into his mind. He had always doubted the existence of the mine, though the discovery of the envelope had carried him away for the moment. A prospector might have any number of reasons for carrying a picture of his cabin in his pocket—but there was still that suggestive letter X, and the mysterious initials, T.A.F. However it turned out, he was certain Ronald was about to write the most important story he had yet handled.

After breakfast Ted set about his regular Saturday morning duties in the yard, which kept him occupied until eleven o'clock. Then he walked the two blocks to Nelson's home, summoning him outside with a well-known whistle. Evincing no undue curiosity, Nelson agreed to let Ronald have his picture of Old Goldie. He secured the negative, and then, having several errands, went along with Ted, stopping at the newspaper office to deliver the picture.

"Talk about your gold mines," said Nelson when Miss Monroe handed him a check for five dollars, "I'm wealthy now."

Nelson's regular allowance usually fell far short of meeting his desires for new photographic supplies. Oddly enough, no one in Forestdale seemed yet to have heard of the death of Old Goldie, and Ronald did not discover the reason until he talked to Ken Kutler several days later.

On Monday Ted found himself to be the man of the hour. Person after person stopped to praise him for the catch he had made, saving their big game of the year, until he sought out Nelson, and complained, "Golly, you'd think I was a hero." But Nelson refused to extend his sympathy.

"You may have a problem, Ted, but I think you'd have a lot worse problem if you'd dropped that ball."

Later that day, while standing in a small group that had been discussing the game, someone exclaimed, "Oh, were you the one who caught that fly, Ted? I forgot." Realizing what a fleeting thing fame is, Ted found his feet planted firmly on the ground once more.

On Tuesday, the appearance of Ronald's story pushed all thought of the baseball game into the background. The sensation which the story created was unparalleled since that last mad "gold rush" to the hills. But although no one had ever found Old Goldie's mine, and the fever had long since died down, it had not disappeared altogether, and only awaited the necessary spark to ignite it once again. Ronald's story had provided the spark, and the streets of town grew quieter as man after man left for the hills. With many of these there was little expectation of sudden wealth, but there was no suppressing the call of adventure. The boys would have liked to follow suit, but the school authorities immediately announced that any students absent without special permission would be expelled at once, putting an end to any plans they may have had.

So the days drifted past, and the boys found their spirits gradually rising as no one reported any success in finding the cabin or the mine, and Ronald, checking regularly at the county court house, was certain that no claim had been filed.

CHAPTER 4

The Return of Jim Rivers

There is no denying the magic lure in the word "gold." It was the same word which sent early explorers to the New World, and later set a mighty nation rushing westward. It called explorers, adventurers, and thieves to the edge of the Arctic Circle, and gallant divers to the bottom of the seas, exploring hulks of once mighty seafaring vessels. It represents generosity, and charity, and adventure, and ambition, and security, and selfishness, and greed. No other word can summarize all that is good and bad in human nature as effectively as the one word, "gold."

Ronald had tried to write his story in as simple and unsensational a manner as possible. He told only the simple facts which were known about Old Goldie, and in connection with the photograph of the cabin he did not mention the gold mine at all. He merely stated that the picture had been found in an envelope with the initials T.A.F. on the outside, and that judging from the shadows on the picture the cabin was probably located on the western slope of some hill.

This was enough. There was no gainsaying the possibilities of that letter X on the tree trunk. The whole town immediately jumped to the conclusion that the cabin was located on the western slope of Thunder Mountain, and that once the cabin was found, the mine itself would not be difficult to find. Since he was not quite sure, Ronald had not mentioned his own theory that the X was on the negative, and not on the tree.

Ted presently discovered that most of his friends fully believed that there was a pine tree with an X carved on it, but he did not trouble to enlighten them. Ronald took pardonable pride in his story, which was spread clear across the front page of the *Town Crier*, along with the pictures of Old Goldie and the cabin. He noted, also, that the North Ridge *News-Record*, which came out on the same day, had only a brief article about Old Goldie, without a word about the photograph, or the initials, or the pine tree. The story had broken in North Ridge, and to have invaded "enemy" territory and snatched a story from under the nose of his rival was a double satisfaction. Yet he knew that it had been the merest chance that he had stumbled upon the story while making inquiries for Ted.

"And I suppose Ken would have done his best to find a blood donor for Mrs. Mulgrew last summer, if he had known about it," Ronald thought. Nevertheless, this time things had fallen his way, and Ken Kutler had been scooped badly. Ken was too good a reporter to take that lying down, and Ronald knew he would have to be particularly alert to make certain Ken didn't find the opportunity to even matters.

That afternoon Ronald was off again to North Ridge. Several new lines of inquiry had presented themselves. He managed to borrow Old Goldie's rock samples for a short time, and took them to a geologist. But the geologist could tell him very little.

"There's no indication of gold, if that's what you mean," he said, looking up at Ronald shrewdly. "These aren't gold-bearing rocks."

"No, I hardly expected that. I was wondering if you could tell me the locality where they were found."

"I'm afraid I couldn't. They're quite common types in this region, of no commercial value at all."

"Then why do you suppose Old Goldie bothered to pick them up?"

"I couldn't say, unless the shapes appealed to him. If you have a good imagination you can suppose they look like animals or things." He shrugged to indicate he didn't have that kind of imagination.

Ronald's next idea was to try to find the photographer who printed Old Goldie's pictures. He entered a drug store, and asked the clerk whether there was any method by which that store's pictures could be identified.

"Yes, there is." The clerk showed him some snapshots which had just been printed. "We stamp an order number on the back of all our prints."

Ronald knew there was no such number on Old Goldie's picture. "Do all commercial studios follow a similar practice?"

"Yes, so far as I know, they all do on work of this kind." Thanking him, Ronald left the store. He had hoped that if the picture had been taken not so very long ago, the clerk who printed it might remember some other pictures on the same roll, which should be of help, but this slender lead had snapped. He realized now that Old Goldie had very likely developed and printed that picture himself.

Although his afternoon's work had availed him nothing, Ronald was glad he had followed out these leads. Another matter was much on his mind.

"You know, Ted, there's someone else who may beat us all to the mine."

"Who is that?" asked Ted, very much interested.

"You remember when we were looking through the file, I mentioned that Old Goldie often went on long trips with the Indian guide, Jim Rivers. It seems to me that if anyone knows the secret of the mine, it is quite likely that Jim does."

"Have you tried to find Jim?" Ted inquired.

"Yes, I have, but I haven't been successful so far. But I did find someone who thinks he knows someone who will know where Jim is. It's a long chance, but it may come through."

"I wonder why T.A.F. hasn't found the mine yet? Do you suppose he never saw the picture in the *Town Crier*?

After all, it's only a little paper—" He ducked quickly as Ronald tossed a cushion in his direction.

Both Ted and his friend Nelson assumed that they would leave for Thunder Mountain at the earliest possible moment. Ted stayed late at Nelson's home one evening while they made the final plans for their expedition.

"There's no school Thursday," Nelson pointed out. "That'll give us a chance to get everything packed up and ready. We'll be out of school by ten-thirty Friday morning, and we'll be on the road by eleven."

"We can go on our bikes," suggested Ted, "as far as the Breckridge farm, and leave them there. I know Mrs. Breckridge won't mind. That will save us a couple hours, and we'll be on the western slope of the mountain by the middle of the afternoon. If we go through Moosehead Pass, that should bring us out right about at Ronald's point." This was the point at which Ronald believed the cabin would be found, on the western slope about half way between Forestdale and North Ridge. If Ronald's theories were right, they would have little trouble finding the cabin— and so, they thought, the mine—if only no one else found it first! But they could not help feeling puzzled that no one had yet found the cabin. Surely the searchers must have covered the western slope of Thunder Mountain rather thoroughly.

"Maybe somebody did find it, and he wants to keep it a secret," suggested Nelson.

"I don't see how anybody could manage to keep a secret like that," maintained Ted. "If I found that mine, I'd rush to the nearest claim office to make sure my claim was filed first."

"But maybe they found the cabin, and not the mine. Maybe the mine isn't going to be so easy to find even after you find the cabin."

Ted shook his head dubiously. "If one person found the cabin, a lot of others could, too, and the secret would be out by now. I feel there's something wrong about this, but we won't be able to tell what it is until we get up to the mountain."

It was late when Ted took his departure, and the streets were dark and pretty well cleared. As he turned off Main Street, and neared the hotel, a man approached him through the darkness, but Ted did not look up until the last instant. Then he gave a gasp of surprise. The man he had just passed was an Indian, and the thought immediately jumped to his mind: "Jim Rivers!"

He turned quickly, but the man had disappeared. Ted retraced his steps to the corner of the street, but there was no sign of the Indian. Reluctantly Ted turned homeward.

Of course he told Ronald about it, who appeared skeptical.

"If it was dark, how can you be sure it was an Indian, Ted.?"

"I don't know. I think he looked up and the light from the street lamp just caught his cheekbone."

"Other people besides Indians have high cheekbones."

"I know, but his skin was rather dark, and I think his hair was black—I'm pretty sure it was an Indian, all right."

"Well, supposing it was an Indian, what makes you think it was Jim Rivers? It's been quite a few years since the last time you've seen him, and you were pretty young then."

"I kind of remember him, though, and he looked just the same. I think it was Jim—but I can't be positive."

The truth was that Ted had never known any other Indian except Jim. Wasn't it natural, then, that encountering an Indian late at night he would assume it was Jim? Memory can be tricky, and Ted found himself growing a little more doubtful.

"If it was Jim that you saw, it seems impossible that anything except the mine could have brought him back to town just at this time. You didn't notice where he went?"

"No, but I have sort of a hunch that he had just come out of the hotel."

"Well, I'll check into it, Ted. Better keep this under your hat until I see if I can find out anything." He checked at the hotel the next day, but Jim Rivers was not listed on the register, and the desk clerk was quite certain that no Indian had been staying there. Then Ronald checked once more with the source he had previously mentioned to Ted, a lumberman who thought he once heard that Jim was associated with another lumber company. This time the lumberman had some news for him.

"Yes, I wrote to my friend I told you about, and he said that Jim had been working for the Cedar Falls lumber mill. That was a couple of years ago, though. He hasn't heard anything about Jim for a long time."

"Then it's possible that Jim is still working in Cedar Falls?"

"Oh, it's possible, all right. If it's important, why don't take a run up and find out about it?"

"Thanks," Ronald returned. "Maybe I will."

But several new assignments had come in for him, and he soon saw that it would be impossible for him to leave town for several more days. He therefore wrote a letter instead. The lumber company replied by return mail. While they were unable to tell him where Jim was just then, they did disclose a few facts which seemed to be of some importance. Although Jim Rivers worked for them, he was not there at the present time, and this unexplained absence only served to convince Ronald more strongly of Jim's involvement in the case. The reporter made several more discreet inquiries in Forestdale, but there was no further news of Jim.

"You would think someone would have noticed Jim if did come here," argued Ted.

"I suppose they would have, if he had been wearing moccasins, an Indian blanket, braids, and a feather in his hair. But Jim would be dressed the same as anyone else, and would attract no special notice, unless a person was close to him. Anyway, I've got the feeling that if it was Jim, he was trying to stay out of sight."

But so far as they could determine no one else had seen an Indian, and as days passed with no further incident it became apparent that if Jim had been in town, he had disappeared again as suddenly as he came.

CHAPTER 5

Who Is T.A.F.?

The small, semi-weekly *Town Crier* hardly represented a reporter's dream. "And yet it's going to be hard to leave," said Ronald with a sigh to Miss Monroe. He sat down on the edge of the desk.

"The office won't seem the same without you, Ronald," said Miss Monroe. She was a number of years older than Ronald, and thus felt at liberty to use his first name, although he always addressed her as Miss Monroe. "I know that Mr. Dobson thinks very highly of you," she went on, "but he wouldn't stand in your way if you saw a chance to better yourself. You really don't belong here—not for very long.

For a reporter there isn't any future on a small paper like this. You'll want to get on a big city paper, if you decide to stay in newspaper work."

"I guess I'll stay, all right," returned Ronald. "There's something fascinating about newspaper work that gets in your blood, and once you've tried it nothing else seems to satisfy you. It's hard work, and it's often a struggle finding stories and beating deadlines, but still it's fun. It gives you a feeling of aliveness, being on the inside of everything important that comes along."

"I know," agreed Miss Monroe. "I suppose your brother Ted wants to be a reporter just like you."

"I guess so. He almost lives and breathes with that school newspaper of his—just as I did at his age." Miss Monroe smiled to herself. She realized that Ted and Ronald were much more alike than they knew. Other people too, recognized many similarities beyond a certain resemblance in build and features—likenesses in gestures and expressions of speech unconsciously copied from each other.

"Are you leaving now?" she asked, as Ronald finally rose from the desk and reached for his notebook.

"Yes. Tell Mr. Dobson I've gone out to the McCatherty place to get the story about his farm award. I'll phone in when I'm done there, and then I'm going to stop over in North Ridge."

"Still working on the gold mine story?"

"Yes, I'm going to see if I can't find someone in North Ridge with the initials T.A.F. Our mysterious friend has to live someplace, and I'm going to try to find out where that is."

This was Wednesday of the week following Ronald's scoop, and the story of the initials had already been reprinted in North Ridge. Thus, wherever he might ask questions, it was pretty certain that people would know what he was after. He decided that a direct approach was best, frankly admitting that he was a reporter working on the Old Goldie story, and hoping for their cooperation.

From the North Ridge directory he had already compiled a list of prospects. It would be impossible for him to call on every family whose name began with F, so he would have to assume that T.A.F. was the head of a family, for other family members were not listed. In Forestdale he had found only two names with the initials T.F., and in each case he had been able to prove that the middle initial was wrong. But in the larger town of North Ridge, he found nearly a dozen T.F.'s, middle initial unknown. It was these names that he proposed to check.

"But will T.A.F. admit he is the right person, even if I find him?" he wondered. Maybe not—but still he thought it worth while to try. Even though T.A.F. might deny his identity, Ronald was a shrewd person, and thought he might be able to guess that something was being concealed.

In most cases his ring was answered by a housewife. Nearly all of them were friendly, although some were obviously busy, and anxious to cut the interview as short as possible. All were curious, and some asked questions, which Ronald answered as briefly as he could. Most were amiable, some reserved, and one or two openly suspicious. But Ronald was diplomatic, and his frank, open manner quickly dispelled any misgivings.

His first difficulty came from a very talkative woman. "You're checking to see if my husband is the T.A.F. who used to know Old Goldie?" Ronald admitted that he was.

"I'm sorry, but he isn't. My husband's middle name is Kriegor, and mine is Janice. Ever since that story appeared people have been asking my husband if he was T.A.F., but he isn't. We've been trying to think back to see if there was anybody in our family named T.A.F., but the closest we could come was an uncle. His name was Thomas Andrew."

"T.A.F.?" asked Ronald, beginning to grow excited. "Oh, no, Thomas Andrew Simmons, that was his name, and I don't think he could have been the one anyway. He lived in England, although his parents came from Bohemia. That was around 1850."

He felt that she would have been willing to supply him with a complete history of all her relatives, but he didn't have time, and in a short while managed to excuse himself. In only one instance did he fail to get the information he desired. At this house he found the man busily mowing his front lawn. Ronald introduced himself, and explained his mission.

"So you want to know my middle initial, and you think I'm going to tell you?" The man's attitude was belligerent.

"It might be to your advantage, as long as you haven't anything to conceal."

"Oh, I haven't got anything to hide, but maybe you have. How do I know you're really a reporter?"

"If you'd care to see my press card—"

"I don't want to see it. It might be forged anyway. For all I know you might be one of those tax agents, snooping around to make sure I've paid all my taxes. Well, you're not going to find out anything from me."

The situation was so obviously hopeless that Ronald soon gave up. Tired, and a little discouraged, he stopped at a restaurant for lunch. He had hardly placed his order when Ken Kutler, the young reporter for the *News-Record*, entered and sat down beside him.

"Well, aren't you a little off your beat, Wilford, or did you come over to get a job on a good paper?"

"Quite the contrary," said Ronald easily. "I came to offer you a job. We could use an office boy."

Interrupting himself long enough to order coffee from the waitress, Ken continued, "Why didn't you tip a fellow off about Old Goldie?"

"Oh, why I thought you would check the hospital lists as a matter of routine."

"I did, and do you know what the idiotic hospital staff did? They had him listed on the register as O.G. Smith. How was I to know that was Old Goldie? The nurse I talked to thought it was a farmer named Smith, who lives way out in the country and has been ill for years. I was too busy to go out just then, so I decided to leave it until the last minute. Then I just barely found out it was Old Goldie in time to get a story in the paper. I talked to Constable Mulgrew about it, and you know something—he never said a word about that envelope until hours past my deadline." He pushed back his chair in disgust. "Honestly, everybody says he's the best chief constable we've had in years, but I don't see how he manages to get by with that poor memory of his."

Ronald tried to conceal a smile. Evidently the constable considered blood to be thicker than water. Ken adopted a friendly attitude which would have disarmed the suspicions of anyone except another newspaper reporter.

"Look here, Wilford, do you know anything about this affair, something you haven't been telling?"

"Who, me?" exclaimed Ronald. "I never know anything until I read it in your paper."

Ken eyed him suspiciously. "All right, Wilford, I didn't expect you to tell me anything. But I'll make a bargain with you. I've uncovered something that I think you don't know about. If I tell you, will you tell me a few things?"

"Well, that all depends," said Ronald cautiously.

"Well, here it is." Ronald sat back to listen. He did not expect that the information which Ken was so liberally giving out would be very important. "Do you remember the Up-State Mining scandal?"

Ronald could recall only vaguely how the firm Up-State Mining Enterprises had gone bankrupt about five years before.

"The partners were engaged in some fraudulent deals," continued Ken. "Jamison and Reegan lit out, but Frederick Fairchild was held for trial. He was found guilty, but received only a suspended sentence, for there were extenuating circumstances. He left town soon after the trial, and I have been unable to find any trace of him since. Reegan and Jamison were picked up later and held on some other charge, and never were returned here for trial."

"Just how does that relate to Old Goldie?" asked Ronald.

"For one thing, Old Goldie often had business dealings with the company, bringing in his supplies of gold to them. I have been checking back over the accounts of Fairchild's trial, and it seems that Old Goldie's name came up several times. The partners led the public to believe they had a claim to that mine Old Goldie was supposed to have. Many people lent money to the company because of this, and of course they lost it when the firm went bankrupt. It was proved at the trial that if Old Goldie did have such a mine, the Up-State company had no claim to it."

Ronald listened carefully to Ken's story, and turned the facts over in his mind. Old Goldie had had some connection with Up-State Mining Enterprises, but this appeared to bear no relation to the fact that the company later went bankrupt. The story was interesting, but, as he had believed before, did not seem to be very important at the present time.

"And now," proceeded Ken, "it's your turn to tell me something. What do you know about this Indian, Jim Rivers?"

Ronald debated carefully. He decided that there would be no harm in telling Ken what he knew about Jim, particularly as he didn't know very much!

"I've discovered," began Ronald, "that Jim Rivers has been working for several years in Cedar Falls as a forest ranger with a lumber company.

His relations with the company were rather loose. The company employed him in a kind of advisory capacity, and they had no objection when he would sometimes leave them for a week or two at a time and go off on some plan of his own.

"After receiving a special delivery letter last Friday night, he left suddenly Saturday morning. That night my brother, Ted, reported seeing an Indian in Forestdale, but he could not be certain that it was Jim, and later I was unable to find any trace of him. All that I know is that Jim Rivers has not yet returned to Cedar Falls."

"Hum, that's interesting," said Ken Kutler. "And now, tell me what you are doing in North Ridge today."

But Ronald decided that he had carried his part of the bargain quite far enough.

"Just trying to make a few new friends," he said casually.

"Isn't it strange?" said Ken. "I happen to know that you called on the Fremonts, the Fultons, and the Farlingtons. Rather strange that all your friends should have names beginning with F. Do you think this fellow T.A.F. is in North Ridge?"

"I like people whose names begin with F," Ronald evaded. "It's just a special little fondness of mine."

"All right, Wilford," said Ken, rising to his feet, "wait till the next big story breaks. I'll scoop you so badly you'll have to retire."

Ken strode out of the restaurant. An onlooker would not have guessed that the two young men were the best of friends.

* * * *

"And that ends that idea," Ronald reported to Ted that evening.

"What about that fellow who wouldn't tell you his initials? Do you think he might be the right one?"

"No, I've thought a lot about it and I don't think so. It seems to me that if he was T.A.F. he would either have admitted it or denied it. I imagine he just wanted to act important. But it's something we have to keep in mind. Actually, I don't think there is any T.A.F. in either Forestdale or North Ridge."

"Maybe T.A.F. is a farmer," suggested Ted.

"Well, the directories covered all the farmers in both townships."

"Then maybe he lives farther out."

"That's possible, I suppose, but Old Goldie's activities were centered around here. Anyway, we can't hope to cover the whole state."

"Ron," said Ted suddenly, "what if T.A.F. is a woman instead of a man?"

"I don't think it's probable. Besides, the single women are listed in the directories, while a married woman would be more likely to use her husband's initials."

"But maybe T.A.F. was her maiden name, and now she's married and has a different name, and there isn't any way to trace her." Ronald thought it over carefully.

"That doesn't sound very likely, but it could happen. We'll have to remember it."

For some reason Ted thought about T.A.F. all that evening, and he must have fallen asleep with that thought on his mind. For during the night he awakened suddenly. His memory went reeling back—a casual incident deeply buried in hidden recesses of his mind, a fragmentary glimpse which struggled to make itself known, was lost, and reappeared again stronger than before. He slipped out of bed, into the hall, and into Ronald's room without knocking.

"Ronald," he said in a loud whisper, "Ron, I know who T.A.F. is!"

CHAPTER 6

A Rebuff

Ted directed the bed lamp full into his brother's eyes.

"Wake up, Ron," he called.

"Go away," murmured Ronald sleepily. "You sound like an electric razor buzzing in my ears."

He opened his eyes suddenly and looked suspiciously at the pajama-clad figure bending over him. "Ted, have you been using my electric razor?"

"Well, I tried it out this morning," admitted Ted. "I'm getting to be quite a man, you know."

"Shucks, fellow, you aren't a man until you can wiggle your ears, like this." Ronald tightened up his facial muscles and managed to move his ears back and forth at a rapid rate. Ted laughed. In his younger years he had never failed to marvel at this accomplishment, which Ronald claimed was evidence of his maturity. But just now he had something more important on his mind.

"Well," said Ronald humorously, "I don't suppose you awakened me at midnight just to see me wiggle my ears. What's bothering you?" Ted explained quickly.

"That day we played North Ridge, Margaret Lake had a little crippled boy with her. I noticed he had his initials on the pocket of his shirt, and I'm almost sure the initials were T.A.F. At least, I'm pretty sure about the T.F."

"Another T.F.!" said Ronald with a sigh. "Listen, Ted, you should have been with me today and seen how many people I found in North Ridge with the initials T.F. What makes you think this little boy is the right one?"

"I don't know," said Ted desperately, "but I just think he is. What do you think?"

"I think," said Ronald with a yawn, "that you're probably mistaken about the initials. F and S often look alike on monograms."

Could he be mistaken about the initials? But Ted had quite a clear picture of that monogram, and he felt sure that he was right.

"So you know a little crippled boy with the initials T.A.S. on his pocket—"

"T.A.F.!" insisted Ted.

"Well, maybe T.A.F. then, and now you think he's the person we're looking for. What do you know about the boy?"

"Well, his name's Timothy," began Ted, and stopped suddenly. Somehow he had felt that he knew Tim rather well, but now he realized that he really knew practically nothing about him. "Anyway, we should be able to find out about him if he's Margaret's cousin, or something."

"Yes, we could do that," agreed Ronald. "However, I'm interested in knowing your theory about Tim. Do you think Old Goldie left the envelope for him, expected him to understand what it meant, and that he could go searching on the mountain for his gold mine and stake out a claim?" Ronald was being facetious.

"No," said Ted slowly, "I guess not." Surely Old Goldie could not have expected eight-year-old Tim to understand the envelope, or to search for the mine, something which was quite impossible at his age and in his crippled condition. "Maybe he couldn't understand about the envelope now, but maybe he will be able to when he's older."

Was there really any connection between Tim and Old Goldie, Ted wondered? It was hard to imagine an association between the weatherbeaten old prospector and the little crippled boy, but it was possible. Perhaps Tim was Old Goldie's son, or more likely his grandson! But when he voiced this suggestion, Ronald did not think much of it.

"Old Goldie doesn't seem to me to be the kind of person who would ever marry, certainly not in the years he has been known around here. And surely if he had relatives in this district more would have been known about him by this time. However, I do think we should have a talk with Mrs. Lake tomorrow. And now how about letting me have a few hours more sleep. I can't think clearly at this hour of the morning."

Ted returned to his own room, but he did not fall asleep immediately. His thoughts turned back to Tim, and he recalled almost every detail of their meeting. He had taken a liking to the little fellow, and wished with all his heart that there was some way he could help him.

There was no school on Thursday, and Ted accompanied Ronald to the Lake home. Margaret was not at home, but Mrs. Lake admitted them, and they sat down in the pleasant living room.

"Our errand here is a little unusual," began Ronald, "and perhaps rather foolish. You know that in connection with this Old Goldie story I have been trying to find a person with the initials T.A.F. Now it seems that several weeks ago, at a ball game, Margaret had with her a little boy named Timothy—your nephew, perhaps."

"No," said Mrs. Lake, shaking her head. "He's not a relative. I only met Mrs. Stoneman recently in connection with some charity work. She was at the head of her committee in Little Rapids, and I had a few questions to ask her." She saw Ted and Ronald exchange significant glances, and looked at them questioningly. Ronald hastened to explain.

"Ted and I had a little discussion about Tim's initials, and it would appear that I was right, for if his mother's name is Stoneman—"

"Oh, but I didn't mean to say Mrs. Stoneman is his mother," Mrs. Lake broke in quickly. "She is his aunt." Ronald was taken aback at this new information, while Ted at once became more cheerful.

"Still, his name might be Stoneman, just like his aunt's," said Ronald.

"Yes, it might," admitted Mrs. Lake. "I really don't know."

"Didn't you notice the monogram on his pocket, Mrs. Lake?" Ted put in.

"I'm afraid I didn't, Ted. I felt so sorry about his leg that I didn't pay any attention to his clothes."

"Isn't there something that could be done for Tim?" asked Ronald.

"I don't know," she said. "Mrs. Stoneman spoke about operation later this summer." As Mrs. Lake could offer no further information, except for Mrs. Stoneman's address in Little Rapids, Ronald wrote it down in his notebook, they thanked her and left.

They climbed back into Jeremiah, which they had endowed with almost human characteristics. There was nothing prophetic intended in the name. Jeremiah was the name of their great-uncle, well known for his obstinacy.

"Well, Jeremiah are we going to get started today?" Ronald had said one cold morning when the car refused to budge, and the name had clung. They would not for the world have thought of keeping anything important from their mother, but this was a private little joke just between themselves.

* * * *

Shortly after eleven o'clock they entered the village of Little Rapids. It was a cozy little community, with everything appearing bright and clean. The streets were bordered by stately elms, and flowers were in abundance.

"What do you say, Ted, shall we have lunch now or see Mrs. Stoneman first?"

"Don't you think we had better go there first? I'd like to see Tim, and he may have a nap after lunch."

They had no difficulty in finding the address. Little Rapids really consisted of only two important streets which crossed each other. As they drove down the cross street and drew up in front of an ivy-covered bungalow, they saw Tim playing in the yard. Ronald stopped the car and Ted stepped to the curb.

"Hello," called Ted. "Do you remember me?"

"Ted!" the little boy shouted eagerly. "Did you come to play with me?"

"Well, I guess I could for a little while." From his pocket Ted produced a bag of marbles they had purchased on the way. The small hands fumbled excitedly at the package, then held the colored balls up to the light with exclamations of pleasure. Obviously the child had not had too many playthings. Ted noticed that there were no initials on the shirt Tim was now wearing.

"I wonder if I could talk to your aunt," said Ronald kindly. He, too, had taken a sudden attachment to the boy.

"I guess so." Tim led them up the broad white steps, stumbling eagerly ahead of them, and into the old-fashioned parlor.

"Aunt Molly," he introduced, "this is my friend Ted who came to play with me." Ronald stepped forward.

"How do you do, Mrs. Stoneman," he began. She acknowledged the remark with a nod and a questioning look. "Mrs. Stoneman, I am a reporter from the Forestdale *Town Crier*. I would appreciate it very much if you would permit me to ask you a few questions." At his words the woman stiffened noticeably.

"Timmy," she ordered sharply, "go into the kitchen and have your lunch."

"But Aunt Molly," the boy protested, "Ted is my friend. He came to play with me."

"Timmy, do as I say," and slowly the boy obeyed. "I'm sorry," she said, turning back to the two young men, "but I never talk to reporters."

"But Mrs. Stoneman, we're Tim's friends. There may something we can do."

"I'm sorry," she repeated, and led the way to the door, as they started to leave she softened a little. "Thank you for being kind to Timmy," she almost whispered.

Once more on the sidewalk, Ted exclaimed, "Whee! We were as welcome there as rain at a picnic. What shall we do now, make some more inquiries?"

Ronald answered slowly, "No, I think not. As long as Tim's a friend of yours I don't quite like the idea of snooping. Anyway, if the Stonemans have anything important to hide it isn't likely the neighbors would know anything about it."

"I guess we weren't very successful. We still don't know for certain if Tim's initials are T.A.F."

"No," Ronald agreed, "but we did find out some things. Did you notice how Mrs. Stoneman said she never talked to reporters? That sounds as though she had been bothered by reporters at some time in the past. Then, too, her refusal to talk to us shows that she knows certain things which she doesn't wish to be made public. Oh, the more I think about it, I am convinced that Mrs. Stoneman could tell us a great deal if she only would, but whether her secret has anything to do with Old Goldie or not I can't say."

"If Tim had been wearing that same shirt, I could prove to you about those initials."

"Memory is a funny thing," put in Ronald. "You were thinking so much about the initials T.A.F. that when you tried to recall the initials on Tim's shirt it may be that the letters T.A.F. came to your mind by the process of association. That would be quite possible, especially since you already knew Tim's first initial. When people try to recall an event they sometimes imagine that it happened the way they would have liked to have it happen, rather than the way it really did happen."

"That sounds kind of involved," said Ted, smiling. "Maybe it is," said Ronald, seemingly rather disappointed over their failure. He turned the car around and they headed back toward Forestdale.

CHAPTER 7

On Thunder Mountain

The closing days of the school term had been busy ones, and would have seemed to pass quickly had it not been for the haunting fear Ted and the other boys shared that Old Goldie's cabin and mine would be found before they could take up the search. But the reports that came back from the mountains were more and more discouraging, and the students became more cheerful.

The fact that final examinations were over, and that most of the students had passed successfully, also contributed to the general feeling of buoyancy. Was there ever a student who did not feel a thrill of expectation on the last day of school? There is the feeling of a coming release from routine, and the taking up of new pleasures, duties, and experiences, and this year the prospective search for Old Goldie's mine promised to make the vacation more exciting than ever. Thus it was on Friday that the sun seemed a little brighter, and the air a little clearer; voices were pitched a little higher, and there was a certain lack of restraint in the conversation.

The final edition of the *Stateman* was released that morning. Ted noted that Margaret's interview had been the one selected for publication. It was prominently displayed on the front page and carried over to an inside page, and as he slowly read the article he realized with what effort and ingenuity Margaret had secured her information and written her story.

His own story had not progressed so satisfactorily. He had been preoccupied with thoughts of Old Goldie and the mine, and the story he finally wrote was based on an informal talk he had had with the mayor. With a true newspaperman's insight, he knew that his interview was only mediocre, but he submitted it as evidence that he had tried the assignment.

Margaret's story, he realized, was much better planned and executed than his had been, and he hastened to congratulate her. Margaret quickly cast his praise aside. She realized that he must be disappointed at having been unable to get the interview he had first planned so hopefully, and she hastened to reassure him.

"I saw your string book on Miss Trisdale's desk this morning," she told him, "and you had more inch credit for the year than anyone else on the staff." Needless to say, Ted immediately felt better.

At the end of the morning's session, he hastily cleaned out his locker and left the building, not stopping to join any of the groups which had gathered outside. After all, it wasn't like a real leave-taking, for most of the students would remain in Forestdale the better part of the summer.

By eleven o'clock he and Nelson were on their bicycles on the road out of Forestdale, their equipment and several days' supplies neatly packed. The road led to the west almost straight ahead for ten miles, when it turned northward and wound around the foot of the mountains toward North Ridge. Ahead of them Thunder Mountain loomed tall and dark, almost foreboding through the haze.

A stranger in town might have thought that Forestdale nestled at the very foot of the mountain, for the town seemed to be overshadowed by the peak, but actually a trip to the mountain was almost half a day's journey on foot. Thunder Mountain was the highest peak in the range of hills that rose from the plains. The range continued to the north, where it dropped abruptly to the town of North Ridge, and to the south it also stretched for miles, finally dwindling back into the plain.

Moosehead Pass was a cut which separated Thunder Mountain from the lesser hills to the south, and provided the best means of crossing the range. There was but little conversation on the trip out, for the road was a steady grade up hill. It was over an hour before they reached the farmhouse, and by then they were glad to rest for a time, sampling the doughnuts provided by the hospitable Mrs. Breckridge.

"Not that I take much stock in that story about a gold mine," she said. "My husband lost a lot of money when that company in North Ridge went bankrupt. We thought they owned Old Goldie's mine, but now I don't think there ever was such a mine." She went back into the house.

"It's about twelve-thirty now," calculated Ted. "It shouldn't take us more than three hours to get through the pass, and that will bring us just about to 'Ronald's point.' We can begin our search from there."

"If our stomachs hold off that long," said Nelson. "I didn't realize how hungry I was until we started eating these doughnuts."

Mrs. Breckridge readily granted them permission to leave their bicycles in the barn. As they talked they removed their supplies from their bicycle carriers. Food for three days, utensils, blankets, and a flash-light formed the bulk of their equipment, and they felt prepared to meet whatever challenge the elements might hurl at them. As they assembled their supplies, Ted noticed that Nelson looked often at the sky.

"What's the matter?" he asked, following Nelson's glances somewhat anxiously. He was reassured by the fleecy wool pack clouds which dotted the heavens.

"Cumulus," said Nelson briefly, referring to the clouds. In connection with his photography, he had made a study of clouds, and took pride in pointing out the various types.

"You mean those innocent white clouds might bring rain?" asked Ted. "Why you can see them on almost any summer day. They just float harmlessly along until the wind drives them away."

"They aren't as innocent as they look," maintained Nelson. "They consist of heavy water vapor, and all they need is a cold current of air to bring about condensation." As he spoke the bright sun was temporarily obliterated by a passing cloud. The possibility of rain did not lessen their enthusiasm for the trip; on the contrary the thought of spending the night on the mountain during a rainstorm suggested adventure.

"Rain might stop a lot of other people from going up the mountain," Ted pointed out, "but it won't stop us. Maybe we won't have as much competition as we thought."

"If it really is going to rain," put in Nelson, "we should be getting on as far as we can." Accordingly bicycles were wheeled into the barn, thirst was appeased at the pump, knapsacks were donned, good-byes were waved to Mrs. Breckridge, and the long trek up the mountainside was begun. The trail did not lead straight up the mountain, but rather veered off to the south toward the pass. It wound through the trees, sometimes very steep, and in other places more level; the exertion of the climb was enough to leave the boys almost breathless.

For other reasons, too, their progress was not as rapid as might have been expected. Nelson had brought his camera with him, and stopped several times to snap pictures of the scenery to add to his already large collection, often delaying their climb for several minutes while he debated various plans of composition.

Ted, too, contributed to the delays. With every cabin they passed, no matter how unlikely, he would draw from his wallet a newspaper clipping showing the picture of Old Goldie's cabin, and carefully compare the scenes. This in spite of the fact that they were still on the eastern slope of the mountain.

Just why he did this he did not know. On this one point they were all agreed; that the cabin must be located on the western slope of some hill or mountain. There were many possible objections to Ronald's theory of the halfway point, or of the running water, but they could offer no other explanation of those shadows on the picture. The shadows had to point, roughly, in a northerly direction, and the cabin had to be located on a western slope. No other theory seemed to meet the facts.

It is probable, however, that neither of the boys was taking the expedition too seriously. Nelson seemed just as intent upon keeping his eye alert for possible photographic subjects as he was concerned about finding the cabin. As for Ted, he was interested in finding the mine just as he was in solving any puzzle, along with the added possibilities, however remote, of sudden wealth and of providing Ronald with a good story, but it is likely that he would not be unduly disappointed if they failed. Hiking was one of his favorite forms of recreation, and in addition there was the thrill of spending several nights on the mountain in cabins found along the way wherever dusk should overtake them. Altogether it was the kind of trip they would probably have undertaken that summer even if Old Goldie's mine had not given their plans a sudden impetus.

For an hour or more the boys followed the long trail leading to Moosehead Pass. They passed among groves of trees and open places, and at one point the trail led over a mountain stream, a fallen log serving as a primitive bridge. Far above their heads they could see a spring bubbling forth from the side of the mountain, the water forming a waterfall into the pool beneath. A sign posted by the state health department announced that the water was safe for drinking. They had been feeling that they had gone miles into the wilderness, but the sign suddenly recalled them to modern civilization.

In truth they did appear to be far from the works of man. The mountain had a look of wild desolation, as though inviolate from white men, and the trail they were following might have been the same as one blazed by Indians five hundred years ago. An occasional rabbit scampered across the path, and squirrels chattered at them from the trees, but they met no people. Altogether it was a lonely place, and inwardly they were glad of each other's company.

From time to time Nelson commented on the changing cloud formations, seemingly taking some delight in the fact that his earlier predictions were being borne out. The innocent-appearing summer clouds had begun to bulge out on top, their sweeping billows proclaiming the formation of thunderclouds, and the sky was darkening ominously.

CHAPTER 8

In the Cabin

Nelson unslung his camera from the case at his side, and in a last burst of sunshine snapped a picture for his cloud collection, a photograph made possible by the use of a yellow filter over the lens. His album was divided into sections, dealing with various kinds of sports, scenes, and activities. He was particularly proud of his cloud collection, which was a novelty, and would have been outstanding had he been able to overcome his perennial lack of funds to purchase different types of filters and special films.

Returning the camera to its case, he said, "I don't really mind getting wet, but it seems to me that we should be looking for shelter," for already large drops were falling, and it was apparent that the shower could not hold off much longer. Ted agreed with this opinion, but where were they to seek shelter, whether up the mountain or down, before them or behind them?

"I noticed a cabin about half a mile back, way above our heads," said Ted. "Maybe we ought to head for there."

There seemed to be no shelter closer at hand, and much as they disliked to retrace their steps, this appeared to be wiser than trusting to the uncertainties of the trail ahead. Accordingly they recrossed the stream and followed another trail leading up the mountainside. After a short climb they reached a level clearing, at the other side of which stood the old cabin barely visible from the trail beneath. They made for this, hurrying faster as the shower increased in intensity. Indeed, by the time they reached the cabin they were thoroughly drenched.

"At least there's no chance of this being Old Goldie's cabin," panted Nelson, glancing to his right as they trotted up the path to the cabin door. "The pine trees aren't here."

"Not to mention its being on the wrong side of the mountain," said Ted, pushing open the cabin door, which was slightly ajar. The cabin in which they found themselves consisted of a single room. To the left was a fireplace, and to the right the frame of a cot, with a corn husk mattress.

A crude table was nailed to the rear wall, in front of the only window, and two homemade chairs and a small cupboard completed the furnishings. Overhead was an open loft, covering about half the room, and reached by a rugged ladder.

They stripped off their streaming garments, wrapped themselves in blankets, and set about the task of cleaning out the fireplace and building a fire. The cupboard yielded some old newspapers, and Nelson was about to use these to start the fire when Ted snatched them from his hand.

"Just wanted to see the dates of the papers," explained Ted. The papers were those from a nearby city, and were about two years old.

"Probably the cabin has been vacant for nearly two years," said Ted, and Nelson, judging from the appearance of things, was inclined to agree. With the papers, some dry leaves, and a few sticks of wood they found in a corner, a fire was started, and soon the aroma of frying potatoes and hot chocolate filled the cabin. This, with the sandwiches they had brought from home, provided a tempting meal, and the boys fell to with a will, their appetites whetted by the exertion of the morning.

"This is the life," said Nelson lazily, when his appetite was fully satisfied. "Wish we could stay right here all summer."

"And let a gold mine slip through our fingers?" demanded Ted. "Nothing doing."

There was no immediate chance of continuing the journey, for the downpour had lessened only slightly. Far from feeling impatient, they rather welcomed the respite. With the remnants of their lunch cleared away, they sat before the fire, warming themselves thoroughly.

As the afternoon wore on, and the rain continued to come down, they began to grow restless. Their clothes were dry, and they dressed themselves again. Fully rested, they were eager to push on their way, but it was five o'clock before the rain let up. Reluctantly they agreed that there was no use continuing that day. The path had turned into mud in many places, and the dark sky meant a possible return of the rains.

A light snack sufficed them for their evening meal, and as they sat around the evening seemed endless. Ted had a pencil and a notebook in his pocket, and for a time kept Nelson engrossed with a little game he was able to win every time, until he explained to Nelson how he did it. After that their attention wandered, and they gave up any pretense at keeping themselves entertained.

"I wouldn't mind the rain," complained Nelson, "except that we've wasted so much time."

"Oh, we've come pretty far on our way," said Ted, trying to put the best possible face on things, "and we can get an early start in the morning."

But he, too, realized that the long shower had upset their plans. They had promised to be home by Sunday afternoon, and now had less than a full day for their search.

"Anyway, it shouldn't take us long to find the cabin," said Nelson, "if it's anywhere near where Ronald said it would be."

"I don't know," said Ted doubtfully. "You'd think someone would have found it before now. But Ronald was sure no one has filed a claim to the mine yet, at least up until last night. You know, I've got an idea that mine isn't going to be so easy to find. Old Goldie wasn't very well educated, but he was a cagey fellow, and he's probably gotten the mine hidden in some way so that it won't be very easy for anyone to get at it."

The cot with the corn husk mattress did not appear very inviting, but they laid out their blankets and prepared to make the best of it. The air was cool, and in spite of the lumps in the mattress they were glad to snuggle down under the covers. Sleep was not long in coming, and the night passed without incident. They were up at break of day, and a breakfast of bacon, potatoes, and hot chocolate put them in the best of spirits for their coming search.

"Today is the day," declared Nelson cheerfully. "Yes," agreed Ted, "today we do it, or we don't."

That was the thought which occupied their minds: Today they would find the cabin, or else—it wasn't going to be easy to find. The fire put out and provisions packed, preparations were soon made for leaving. But somehow Ted found himself a little reluctant to start out.

"You know," he said, "when we first ran in here yesterday a sudden feeling came over me for an instant as though I should know this place— as if I had been here once before. It was just a flash and then it was gone."

"Maybe you were here once before," suggested Nelson. "No, I'm quite sure I wasn't," said Ted, shaking his head. Nelson took out his camera.

"At least we'll always have a picture to remember this adventure. There's something awfully picturesque about a lonely cabin like this one, isn't there?"

Ted agreed, and they took up their bundles and started out across the clearing. But Ted lingered a little behind Nelson, and several times turned to look back at the dilapidated old cabin. Then he shook his head and followed his friend down the path.

CHAPTER 9

Discovery at Moosehead Pass

The sun came out bright that morning, and soon had erased all traces of the preceding day's shower, except in the deep gulches or beneath the umbrella of overhanging limbs where its hot rays could not penetrate. Ted and Nelson followed the path down the mountain to the point where it joined the original trail, and they took to this once more, pursuing it across the mountain stream and on upward in the direction of Moosehead Pass.

The footing was uncertain in places, but this was all part of the spirit of adventure, and added to the fun. No cares weighed upon their youthful shoulders. The spirit of vacation was too new upon them to permit them to become discouraged over the slight delay. What if they didn't find the mine? They still had the fresh mountain air, the returning sunshine, enough good food to satisfy their palates, and at least another day of carefree rambling over the mountainside. What more could they ask?

If they had been older they might have thought of several other things—success, prestige, and worldly possessions—but these would have been a poor exchange, for none of them would have been worth one hour filled with the pure zest for living. Of course it would be nice to find the mine, too, and have all the small boys in town point after them and say in a loud whisper, "Look, they're the boys who found Old Goldie's mine. They look just like ordinary people, don't they?" And the older folks would be proud to stop them on the street and talk with them, and they might have allowances of as much as a dollar a week to spend as they chose.

But all this was boyish fancy, and not to be confused with the actual thrill of communing with nature's great outdoors again, of exercising muscles grown soft through winter months, and of returning once more to the mountain, their own dominion. For coming back to Thunder Mountain was like coming home again, so much was the mountain a part of their lives.

Starting way back when they were too young to make the trip alone and had to tag along with the older boys— when they could—they had spent a part of each summer on Thunder Mountain, hiking, exploring, climbing, camping. During the school year the trip was too long to make except on very special occasions, but still Thunder Mountain was not lost to them. Each day they looked upon this challenging peak that hovered over the town and longed for the time to come when they could return again to its friendly slopes.

It took them more than an hour to reach the eastern entrance to Moosehead Pass. The floor of the pass was about half as high above the plains as was the mountain peak itself, and offered the easiest method of crossing the range for miles in either direction. At the end of the passage, mounted on the southern hill, was a cabin, seemingly standing guard as a sentinel over the trail; but there was no sign of life. They did not stop to explore, but pushed on through the pass. The pass was not a straight cut, but turned several times, and high cliffs encompassed the boys on all sides, as though closing in upon them and threatening to hold them prisoner.

Fifteen minutes of steady hiking brought them to the western terminus, where a magnificent spectacle awaited them. From their point of vantage they could see almost the entire western slope of Thunder Mountain, as well as lesser hills to the north veering off toward the west, while the plains spread out below them like a patchwork quilt, disappearing into the misty horizon.

"Oh boy!" exclaimed Nelson, thinking of what a wonderful picture it would make, but realizing how completely inadequate his camera would be to record such a scene. Ted looked on in appreciative silence. But Nelson's quick eye soon discerned something else more immediate importance to them, tiny specks swarming over the hillside like ants.

"Guess we have some competition, he observed.

"There must be at least a dozen other parties on the mountain," said Ted.

"Looks more like twenty to me," claimed Nelson. "Must be a hundred people all together."

They had expected to meet other parties, it is true, but they were hardly prepared to find so many of them. The enthusiasm among the adults for the search had died out in the past two weeks, and their places had been taken by students who had been held in leash so far only by the strict discipline of the school authorities.

"As nearly as I can figure out," said Ted, "we are just about half way between Forestdale and North Ridge, judging walking standards," and

Nelson nodded his agreement. This then, was "Ronald's point," the place where Ronald had said the cabin should be found.

They began the search from there, continuing on toward north. For the most part it was not necessary to separate, for the slope was rather open, although occasionally one of them would diverge into a bypath to make sure that no cabin lurked among a group of trees. A whistle signal served to unite them if they became separated. Each cabin they discovered was carefully scrutinized and compared with the picture. Any cabin which had windows in front was immediately rejected, as were cabins facing directly north or south.

As part of his equipment Ted had brought along a pair of field glasses, which sometimes saved them side trips to observe out-of-the-way cabins. For two hours they pushed onward, sometimes up hill and sometimes down, but always in the general direction of north. By no stretch of the imagination could any of the cabins they found have been Old Goldie's.

At noon they stopped for lunch beside a stream, and considered their situation. They were now closer to North Ridge than they were to Forestdale by several miles, and if there was anything at all in Ronald's theory there was no use in pushing the search farther in that direction.

"I don't want to sound discouraged," said Nelson, contentedly munching a sandwich, "but I can't see much use in exploring on Thunder Mountain any more. We thought we knew just about where the cabin is, and that somehow everyone else had overlooked it, but that doesn't seem to be true. The search has been going on for almost two weeks, and with all the people on the mountain every foot of this whole slope must have been covered. The cabin hasn't been found, so that can only mean that it isn't here."

"Or else that it wasn't recognized," put in Ted. "That cabin may have changed a lot since that picture was taken. Maybe someone even cut a window in the front."

"Or maybe Old Goldie moved the cabin to the other side of the mountain after taking the picture," said Nelson facetiously.

"Or it may have burned down or the wind blown it away," said Ted cheerfully. "We may as well consider all the possibilities."

Nelson, serious once more, said thoughtfully, "I wonder if we couldn't be mistaken about the cabin being on the western slope. Let's look at the picture once more."

Ted produced the newspaper clipping, and they examined it carefully in every detail. The slope of the land proved beyond a doubt that the cabin faced down hill, and the character of the shadows was evidence that it must also face almost west. They knew the general contour of the eastern slope, and while there were various abutments on which a cabin could face either north or south and down hill, they knew of no place where a cabin could face both west and down hill. Therefore the cabin had to be on the western slope.

"Then that must mean the cabin isn't on Thunder Mountain at all," Nelson decided.

"That's strange," exclaimed Ted, "because everyone was so sure it would be. But if it isn't on Thunder Mountain, then it must be either on the hills to the north or the hills to the south."

"The hills to the north toward North Ridge are more likely," suggested Nelson, "but it would take a week to explore them."

A new thought came to Ted. "Look, those hills to south, as you follow them you get farther away from both Forestdale and North Ridge. That would all fit in with Ron's theory, for almost any point on the western slopes of these hills would be about half way between the two towns."

The idea had never occurred to the boys, but now that they stopped to think about it they knew it was true.

Moosehead Pass came out at a point just about half way between Forestdale and North Ridge, and by going south, away from both towns, and distances would remain about the same.

"Anyway for a couple of miles," Ted pointed out. "After that you'll be getting closer to some of the little towns down that way."

Nevertheless, they realized that it was impossible to undertake a search to the south that day. "We'll have to come back soon," said Ted, "and plan on staying at least a week. The other parties have already begun to spread the search to the other hills."

"And if we don't find it to the south, we can go on and search the northern hills," concluded Nelson. With half a day before them, they decided that they might as well continue the search on Thunder Mountain, in spite of their growing conviction that the cabin would not be found there. Accordingly they began to work south again, but this time at a lower level, continuing the careful search they had begun to make that morning.

By late in the afternoon they were back again at Moosehead Pass, more certain than ever that the cabin would not be found on Thunder Mountain.

"Remember that cabin we saw at the other end of the pass?" asked Ted. "We can stay there for the night and return home early tomorrow morning."

This was agreeable, and they proceeded through the pass in silence. They were tired and perhaps a little discouraged, but it was not the kind of discouragement that means defeat. Old Goldie's cabin and the mine were still not found, and until they were the boys felt that their own chances were as good anyone else's. Everything considered, their expedition was not a complete failure. The cabin was certainly not within the limits they had explored, and they felt certain it was not on the mountain. Having eliminated this territory, the southern hills seemed much more promising as an object of a future expedition.

There was another incidental gain from the expedition, too, for Nelson had exposed three rolls of film to add to his collection. Arriving at the other end of the pass, they quickly found the cabin, and mounting up to it they pushed in the door, which opened easily at their touch. They threw down their bundles, preparing to make themselves at home for the night. Nelson volunteered to make a fire, and it was while bending to this task that he gave a sudden exclamation.

"Feel these," he ordered Ted, who had run to his side. Ted touched the coals in the fireplace and discovered that they were still warm. "Someone's had a fire here not many hours ago."

There was other evidence, too, that the cabin had been occupied. A blanket in good condition was flung across the bunk There were newspapers, too, recent ones, and it was while rummaging through these that Ted gave a startled cry, and held aloft an oblong object. It was a Mother Goose book. He opened the book, and on the flyleaf, printed in pencil characters, he read the inscription: "To Tim from Old Goldie."

CHAPTER 10

End of the Trip

Nelson was almost as much surprised as Ted at the sudden discovery, although he did not grasp its real significance.

"Gosh," he said, "do you think Old Goldie left that book here?" Ted shook his head.

"This book proves there is really some connection between Tim and Old Goldie."

"Tim?" asked Nelson. "Who is he?" Ted explained briefly about the little crippled boy.

"I was almost sure Tim's initials were T.A.F., but Ronald didn't think so."

"And you couldn't find out anything more about him?"

"No," said Ted, "his aunt refused to talk with us. We didn't really have anything to go on at the time, but now we have. We are sure that Tim and Old Goldie knew each other."

"If it's the same Tim," suggested Nelson cautiously. "Oh, it must be," asserted Ted. "There could hardly be two of them in this case."

"But how did Tim's book get up here?" wondered Nelson. Neither of them could offer any explanation.

"Listen," said Ted in a hushed whisper, "you don't think this could be Old Goldie's cabin, do you?" With one accord they rushed outside and surveyed the cabin intently. Then they shook their heads. The cabin had two large front windows, it faced toward the north, there were no pine trees in front, the slope of the land was wrong, and the cabin was larger than the one shown in the picture. This cabin could not possibly have been Old Goldie's.

Sadly they reentered the cabin. Ted picked up the book again. Although it showed signs of much use, it was in good enough condition, and still carried its original jacket. He leafed through the book carefully, but could find nothing which would seem to be of help to them. There were no other notations anywhere, and the only possible clue was the various smudged finger marks which suggested that the volume was a child's valued treasure.

"Oh, let's get out of this place!" exclaimed Nelson suddenly. "It makes me feel creepy. I wouldn't be able to sleep a wink here tonight."

They looked at each other. In truth, neither of them felt any desire to spend the night in that cabin. They knew that it was the moral law of the hills that travelers could utilize any shelter they might find, but they could not escape the feeling that they were trespassing. Besides, their discovery of the Mother Goose book was likely to prove embarrassing if the original occupant of the cabin should return.

"We could stay in that same cabin where we were last night," suggested Ted.

"It's still early," Nelson pointed out, "only about five. If we start now we can still get home before dark."

They were tired, for they had been hiking since early morning, but the comfort of sleeping in their own beds would more than compensate for the added exertion of getting home that night. At once they set about getting their things together. It did not occur to Ted to take the Mother Goose book with them, but it did to Nelson, who objected when Ted replaced where he had found it.

"No," said Ted slowly, "I don't see how we can take it."

"But we should give the book back to Tim," argued Nelson.

Still Ted shook his head.

"We don't have any idea how the book got here," he objected.

"But he couldn't have brought the book here himself."

"No," agreed Ted, "the trip would be impossible for him, even with an older person."

"Then the book must have been stolen!" declared Nelson. But Ted still refused to take the book, and Nelson, although not agreeing with the moral point involved, decided that after all it was best they should leave no trace behind them of having visited the cabin. Although deciding to leave the book behind, Ted gave it another thorough examination before stuffing it back under the newspapers. There was no doubt in his mind that the inscription had been written by Old Goldie himself, for the penciled characters were similar to the initials on the back of the envelope.

With their bundles assembled, they started out, hurrying perhaps a little faster than they would have done under other circumstances. For ten minutes they walked rapidly along in silence. Ted was not the kind of boy given to imagining vague dangers, but his senses were keyed up just a little more than were Nelson's, and as they walked along he found himself strangely troubled. He caught himself listening intently, exactly for what he did not know.

Suddenly he whirled about, and thought he saw a shadow flicker across the path. Was there someone standing behind the trunk of that tall pine tree? In the failing light his vision was uncertain, and he could not be sure.

"What is it?" asked Nelson sharply.

"Oh, nothing, I guess," and he started down the path, Nelson following wonderingly. They reached the Breckridge farm by eight o'clock, and their gnawing hunger was partly appeased by the cookies and milk which Mrs. Breckridge insisted upon their having. They rested for half an hour afterward.

"It's too bad we couldn't find the cabin," said Nelson as sat on the lawn, "but sometimes I wonder about Ronald," and he shook his head.

Ted dived upon him suddenly and pinned his shoulders to the ground. Nelson was heavier than Ted, and could probably have thrown him had he chosen, but he was too tired to resist, and anyway it was more fun to pretend to be overpowered.

"Now what was that remark about Ronald?" asked Ted threateningly.

"Oh, I was only going to say, I wouldn't be surprised if he made up this whole thing himself just to give himself a story. Now let me up."

The brief tussle rather than tiring them further, had the effect of buoying up their spirits. Thanking Mrs. Breckridge for her kindness, they mounted their bikes and started back toward town. This time they had a down grade, and they made the most of it. The rushing wind felt pleasant against their cheeks.

"We're going to draw for lunch partners for the junior picnic next week," shouted Nelson against the sound of the wind. "Who do you hope you get?"

"It doesn't make any difference to me," returned Ted indifferently.

"Not much it doesn't," said Nelson. "You're hoping you get Margaret Lake." Ted speeded up his bicycle, not wishing Nelson to see the rising color in his cheeks. There are disadvantages in having an intimate friend who can sometimes guess your innermost thoughts.

They made good time into town, arriving just as the gathering twilight settled into night. They parted at the corner of Nelson's street, promising to get together to compare notes the following evening. Upon reaching home Ted did not retire immediately, for he had been keyed up into a high state of tension all day, and in spite of the fact that he was approaching the point of exhaustion, it was necessary that he should relax before sleep would come to him.

A bath, removing all traces of mountain grime, served to refresh him. Dressed in pajamas, robe, and slippers, he helped Ronald stage one of their familiar refrigerator raids, and while they leisurely nibbled on everything in sight which appealed to them, Ted recounted the experiences of the trip. Ronald sat chagrined while Ted, not opposed to having a little fun on his own account, carefully pointed out, with appropriate comments, the error Ronald had made in calculating the location of the cabin. But when he came to the part about the finding of the Mother Goose book, Ronald was all attention.

"Hum, that is important," said Ronald. "I thought that Mrs. Stoneman might have had some personal reason of her own for not wanting to talk with us, but now it looks like everything is all connected with this case."

"And I must be right about Tim's initials." said Ted eagerly.

"I don't know, but it wouldn't surprise me if you were. At least we know definitely that there was some relationship between Tim and Old Goldie, but we still don't know what their connection was. I don't suppose you happened to notice when that Mother Goose book was published."

"No," said Ted, taken a little aback, "I didn't. Is that important?"

"It might have been of some help in establishing the time when Old Goldie and Tim knew each other. At least it must have been within the last eight years, if Tim is only about eight years old!"

"The book didn't look very new," said Ted. "I would say it was a few years old."

"Did you notice the book's publisher?" asked Ronald. "Yes, I did notice that, because it was published in this state, by the Beaver Publishing Company in Stanton. Is that going to help us?"

"It might. It's just barely possible that the publishers might have some record of the sale, but it's a very long chance. If only we knew who had occupied that cabin where the book was found!"

"With night coming on, we didn't care to stay around and find out," said Ted drily.

"Well, I can't say that I blame you," said Ronald, "but still if we knew that, it might be that the whole case would be solved. I'm beginning to think that that book may turn out to be very important, perhaps in some way serving as a guide to the location of the mine. You suggested once before that Old Goldie may have left some kind of message which Tim would understand when he is older, and it may be that the book forms a part of the message, which Tim will know about when he is old enough to look for the mine himself."

It struck Ted that Tim might never be able to search for the mine himself, but this idea was one which he did not express. Instead he said thoughtfully, "If this is true, then the mine must be very well hidden, for Old Goldie wouldn't want anyone to find it ahead of Tim."

"You're probably right," agreed Ronald. "I also believe Nelson was right when he said the book was stolen— probably by someone who guessed at least part of the secret."

Fifteen minutes later, at midnight, Ted went upstairs and tumbled into bed, thoroughly played out. But even yet he did not fall asleep immediately. He found himself thinking deeply about the events of the trip, and especially pondering one point: Had they been followed after they left the cabin? He was aware that on dark nights or in lonely places people will often imagine that someone is following them, but he did not believe his own reaction fell into this category. His opinion was based on small things: slight sounds he had heard, that shadow across the path, and the possibility of a person's hiding behind that pine tree. He did not believe in saying such things unless he was sure, but a thought, one which he could not put into words, persisted in his mind.

"No white person could have trailed us like that. If we were followed, and I believe we were, it must have been an Indian—Jim Rivers!"

CHAPTER 11

On the Trail of Mother Goose

Nelson came over Sunday night, and once more they reviewed the events of their trip. Undiscouraged by their failure they determined to return as soon as possible to search the southern hills. But several things caused them to decide to postpone the trip for a week. The long stay they now planned on the mountain would require more preparations than did their former expedition, and in addition neither of them wanted to miss the junior picnic on Thursday. The certainty of fun at the picnic was a more alluring prospect than the very doubtful possibility of their finding Old Goldie's cabin.

As a result of his talk with Ronald, Ted was not surprised when, at ten o'clock the next morning, Ronald dashed into the house calling loudly for him.

"Up here," shouted Ted from above. Ronald bounded up the stairs, taking some of them two and a half at a time, with unpleasant results to his shins. He arrived upstairs breathless but whole.

"You're coming with me," he ordered. "Better throw some pajamas into my case because we may be gone over night."

"Sure thing, but where are we going?"

"Goose hunting."

"Goose hunting!" echoed Ted.

"Yes, I'm going to track down Old Mother Goose, and I thought you might want to come along." After explaining to their mother, who smilingly waved them on their way, they soon found themselves on the open road headed toward Stanton.

"I only hope this isn't another wild goose chase," said Ronald, and Ted smiled dutifully at the pun. Once they were out of town, Ted, to his delight, was allowed to take the wheel. Having had a driving course in high school, he had been able to secure a temporary driver's license, and was a competent driver on the lightly traveled highway.

"How does she handle?" asked Ronald, settling himself back comfortably for the drive. In spite of the nickname they had fastened on the car, they still referred to it as "she," an inconsistency which did not occur to either of them.

"Fine!" declared Ted, "but she seems to have a slight rattle in the left fender." The sad truth is that Jeremiah, after years of faithful service, and at the ripe old age of thirteen, showed unmistakable signs of advancing age, and each new symptom of her decline was a source of concern.

"I thought you wouldn't be able to get away right now," said Ted.

"I can't," returned Ronald. "I'm on business. A state senator is introducing an important farm bill in the legislature, and I have an interview with him this evening. When I heard about it, I jumped at the chance. Otherwise I couldn't have afforded to take time out to trace the Mother Goose book, and those things are always unsatisfactory when you try to handle them by mail."

"But do you think we will be able to discover anything?" asked Ted.

"No, I don't, but it's worth trying."

The drive to Stanton would have been uneventful had not Jeremiah developed a new series of coughs, sputters, and knocks. Ronald was much concerned, and when they reached the city he drove to a garage where Jeremiah could receive her much needed attention. It was past the middle of the afternoon by the time they found the office of the Beaver Publishing Company. Ronald explained his mission to a secretary, who in turn referred him to a clerk, an obliging young man.

"I am a reporter for the Forestdale Town Crier," Ronald explained. "A few weeks ago an old prospector died, and no one has been able to learn anything about his identity. However, we did manage to learn one thing, that he once purchased a Mother Goose book. Is there any way you might be able to help us identify this man?" They waited anxiously for the clerk's answer.

"That's a pretty big order," said the clerk, smiling, "and I don't know that I can help you. You see, we sell a great number of books through retail stores throughout the country, while a much smaller part of our business is done by direct mail. If the book was purchased through a store, we would have no record of the sale, but if it was purchased directly we should have an invoice. In what town did the prospector live?"

"Well, he was out on the mountains most of the time," explained Ronald, "but if he ordered the book by mail, it would probably have been sent either to North Ridge or to Forestdale."

The clerk said thoughtfully, "We don't have a regular outlet in either of those towns, although the stores sometime order our books in small quantities, so there's a good chance that this sale was made by mail." He led them to the accounting room, where machine seemed to be going at a rapid rate. Several girls were busy at machines punching holes in cards, which were later used to make the accounting reports. Another employee was standing over an electrically-operated machine which was printing a report. She looked up at their entrance.

"Miss Greene," asked the clerk, "can you show us the sales cards for the Mother Goose book we published several years ago?" Miss Greene opened two small file drawers in which cards were neatly packed. Ted gave a gasp of surprise, for the drawers must have contained about five thousand cards.

"It would take a week to go through those cards," he declared.

"So it would," said Miss Greene with a smile, "if we had to go through them by hand, but we have a machine to do that for us."

"Will you sort these on columns forty-seven and forty-six," requested the clerk, "pulling out all the fifty-fives. Fifty-five is our code number for the North Ridge sales territory," he explained to Ted and Ronald. "She will be able to find a card for every sale of the Mother Goose book in that territory."

Miss Greene took a stack of cards over to a long machine with thirteen different pockets, and started the cards running through. Ted marveled at the swift and unerring manner in which the machine skillfully sorted the cards. Most of the cards went into the reject box, although quite a number went into the five pocket. A minute later he marveled again, for the reject box was almost full, and as Miss Greene had turned away for another task the machine stopped of its own accord. Then Miss Greene removed some of the cards, and the machine started again.

She continued to feed cards into the machine, until all of them had been run through. Several hundred cards had gone into the five box, and these she had to run through the machine again, sorting on the next column. Of these some fifteen cards again entered the five box, and these she handed to the clerk. He thanked her, wrote down a number from each of the cards, and they left the room. The entire process had taken hardly ten minutes.

"Now we can look up the invoice numbers on each of these cards, and see to whom each of the sales was made." The sales had been made about six years ago, so the invoices were not to be found in the regular file room. He led them upstairs to a dusty attic room, and taking down several large books, he looked up each invoice in turn. Several of the sales had been made to North Ridge and Forestdale stores, most of the others had been made out in the names of women, and a couple were to persons of whom they knew. All these could be eliminated.

One remaining name stood out, that of "J. Westlock."

"That must be the one," declared Ronald with deliberate restraint. "Do you have any other information about this man?"

"Not very much. The order came in by mail, and was accompanied by the proper remittance. The book was mailed to North Ridge in care of general delivery, to be left until called for."

Thanking the clerk sincerely for the valuable assistance he had given them, they made their way back to the street. Ronald was jubilant.

"That was a lucky chance," he said. "Now we know that Old Goldie's name was J. Westlock."

"If he used his right name," said Ted doubtfully.

"Oh, more than likely he did. Of course he never told anyone his real name, but on the other hand he never invented a false one, either. I've learned that when you ask people a question they think is too personal, either they tell a lie, or they refuse to answer. Old Goldie didn't lie."

"But even if that is his name, we still don't know much more about him than we did before." Ronald refused to let his enthusiasm be quelled.

"Oh, I don't know. After the story is printed someone who recognizes the name may come forward. I can ask other papers to check the name in their files. Perhaps one of the news services will pick up the story, and then the facts about Old Goldie will be printed in papers all over the country."

They recovered Jeremiah, whose assorted aches and pains had been taken care of. Then they stopped in a cafeteria, their healthy appetites requiring more than the usual satisfaction because of their light lunch at noon. Ronald went for his interview that evening, leaving Ted to explore the city.

He had only been in Stanton on a few occasions before, and had never had the opportunity of wandering about at his pleasure. It was a warm evening, and he was glad to stroll up and down the strange streets, looking into unfamiliar store windows, and reveling in the bustle of activity which was so different from the small town in which he lived.

He met Ronald later at the Y.M.C.A., where they took a room for the night. It was still early, and they had time for an exciting series of games of table tennis in the gym.

"I guess I'm out of practice," said Ronald, as Ted drove the ball into the far corner for his twenty-first and winning point.

"I have been playing quite a bit with Nelson," said Ted modestly, nevertheless accepting his victory with enthusiasm. Like most younger brothers, he had, through the years, grown accustomed to being defeated by Ronald in almost every kind of competition in which they engaged, but lately, as he approached maturity, he discovered that his defeats were becoming less and less certain, and he could often turn them into victories by enthusiastic, heads-up playing. Consequently, he always gave

Ronald a hard battle, taking pleasure in the thrill of a hard-contested game, and the victories that came his way were doubly satisfying.

Later that evening, when they were up in their room, Ted stood looking out the window at the deepening twilight and the flickering lights.

"You know," he said, staring out into the night, "I feel different about Old Goldie now. He wasn't all alone after all. There was someone he cared very much about, and that person was little crippled Tim."

CHAPTER 12

Ronald Is Scooped

Early the next morning, after a hearty breakfast, they took to the road again. Jeremiah appeared to be in much better health, and chugged along contentedly on the long drive home. They did not return directly to Forestdale, but stopped off in North Ridge.

"There is just a very small chance that the postmaster will remember Old Goldie's calling for that package," explained Ronald. They were in a holiday mood. For Ted any kind of traveling was appealing, especially on one of the rare occasions when he was helping Ronald follow up a story. Ronald, also, was in high spirits, for his interview had been a successful one, and in addition he felt that they had made important progress on the Old Goldie story.

"You know," said Ronald, boasting just a little, "this is the first important fact anyone has ever discovered about Old Goldie. It looks like I got a little ahead of Ken Kutler again, and whenever I can do that twice within a month, I'm doing pretty well."

They stopped at the North Ridge post office, but Ronald was unable to discover anything new. It was unlikely that anyone would remember a package called for six years previously, and the fact that new clerks had replaced the former ones made the task impossible.

"We really couldn't have expected anything else," said Ronald. He looked up the name J. Westlock in an old North Ridge directory, but it was not listed, and this, too, added to his belief that Old Goldie and J. Westlock were the same person. Ronald stopped again to purchase a copy of the *News-Record* which had Just been released, and brought the copy back with him to the car. He glanced at the front page, and then suddenly threw the paper down in disgust.

Ted picked up the paper and climbed into the car next to Ronald, who was sitting disconsolately over the wheel. Ted glanced at the paper and caught his breath in a quick gasp as he saw the headline:

OLD GOLDIE'S IDENTITY REVEALED

"You may as well read me the whole thing," said Ronald gloomily. "I only saw the first few lines."

Ted read: "Old Goldie's real name was John Westlock, and he was the son of a wealthy New England banker. This information became known as a result of a long investigation by Kenneth Kutler, reporter for the *News-Record*.

"Found in Old Goldie's possession was a wedding ring on which the inscription 'MASS June 7, 1873' was still visible. Kutler believed that the first word stood for the State of Massachusetts, and that the marriage of Old Goldie's parents had taken place in that state.

"Kutler requested newspapers in some of the larger cities in Massachusetts to check the marriage license files for that date and to furnish him with any information they had in their files about those couples.

"A Boston paper, cooperating gladly, reported that John Westlock and Virginia Murdock were married in Boston on that date, and that they later had a son who might have been Old Goldie. Westlock came from a well-known Puritan family, and was the head of a large banking and investment firm, while Miss Murdock's family had been prominent in politics. The marriage occasioned considerable public notice at the time.

"Further checking of old clippings revealed that the boy, John, at the age of fourteen, became involved with the police, and was sentenced to two years in a boys' reform school. When he was released he immediately ran away from home, and presumably came west. What happened from that time until he appeared in this county many years later is not known, but it is believed that he traveled through the country as a prospector most of the time.

"The investigation leaves little doubt that the person who later became known as Old Goldie was the son, John. He was the heir to a large fortune which he never claimed."

Ted and Ronald sat for a moment in silence regarding the story of the man they had known so well and about whom they had known so little.

"Then there was a reason after all for Old Goldie's strange behavior," said Ted at last.

"I guess there was," agreed Ronald, feeling a wave of pity sweep over him for the old prospector. Recalling himself to the more immediate present, he added, "But I wish I had been the one to find it out instead of Kutler."

"At least you had Old Goldie's name," Ted pointed out, "and you might have had all this other information within a week."

"Huh, a story a week late is as good as no story at all. No, I've been scooped good and proper." He slapped his knee reflectively. "But I'll certainly have to give Kutler credit. He used his head in tracking down that inscription, and he stuck with his story until he had it. Well, that settles it. Now we simply have to find that gold mine. I won't be able to hold my head up again in town until we do."

Ronald started the car and they headed back toward Forestdale. "The trouble is I don't quite know what to do next. Everywhere we turn we run up against a blank wall. People have been hunting for that cabin for weeks and still it hasn't been found. Mrs. Stoneman refused to tell us whatever it is she knows. Jim Rivers is still missing, or at least he hasn't returned to Cedar Falls. And there is that person T.A.F. We think it might be Tim, but we don't know for certain."

"How about that cabin where we found the Mother Goose book?" suggested Ted. "Do you think we might discover something if we went back there?"

"Mm—no, I don't think so. The occupant of the cabin is probably gone by now, and even if he's still there he would probably refuse to answer our questions. No, I think our only hope is to find Old Goldie's cabin, but where it is or why it hasn't been found already I can't understand."

"We're planning another expedition next week," offered Ted. "We want to explore the southern hills."

"Well, it might be there," agreed Ronald, "and I hope you find it. But people have been exploring those hills already, and hang it, I still have the feeling that the cabin should be on Thunder Mountain. Everything points that way." He added somewhat grimly, "I don't really care who finds the cabin, but I want the story before Kutler gets it."

He dropped Ted off at their home, and drove on back to the office. Ronald was feeling very discouraged, more so than he had cared to let Ted know. For weeks he had tracked down every possible clue (overlooking the wedding ring, it is true) and still he was no closer to finding Old Goldie's cabin or his gold mine than he had been on the very first day. He had built up his theory carefully, and he was so sure that the cabin would be easily found from his description. Now that weeks had passed and he had exhausted every clue, he felt frustrated, as a reporter always feels when he knows there is a good story but he is unable to get it.

Thursday was the day of the junior picnic, and Ted discovered that Margaret Lake was to be his lunch partner.

Whether this was a pure coincidence, or whether it was due to the fact that Nelson had served on the arrangements committee, he never learned. There was another possibility which did not occur to him, that Margaret might have done a little maneuvering on her own. In any case, they were both well satisfied.

The feature of the picnic was a baseball game between the boys and the girls. The contest was a close one, chiefly because the boys were required to bat left-handed, and it was not surprising that the girls managed to eke out a narrow victory in the five innings played. After that there was boating on the lake and rambling walks through the woods. They returned home in the early evening, tired but content.

Saturday night found Ted and Nelson in Nelson's basement, where he had his dark room. Nelson had already developed the three rolls of film he had exposed on their trip, and he invited Ted over to print the pictures.

"Twenty-four pictures," said Nelson, "and I want two or three prints of each, so that ought to make a good evening's work." Ted's knowledge of photography was limited, but he was eager to learn.

"Just pretend I don't know anything," he said with a grin, "and you won't be far from wrong."

"There isn't much to it," said Nelson, closing the door of the dark room and turning on the small red bulb by which they were to work. "I thought you could print them while I handle the baths."

He showed Ted how to fit the negatives into the frame and hold them up to the light, which was then turned on for a few seconds. "About three seconds should be right," said Nelson. Accordingly Ted began exposing the negatives, holding them to the light, which passed through the negative and affected the paper beneath. Then he handed the papers on to Nelson, who placed them in the developing bath.

"These seem to be coming out rather good," said Nelson a little later, examining the prints as he took them from the developer. He rinsed them in clear water and placed them in the fixing bath.

"Which side of the negative did you say should be facing the light?" asked Ted.

"The glossy side."

"I'm not sure I did that all the time," said Ted. "What happens if I had the other side up?"

"Then the picture will be backwards," explained Nelson. "But it doesn't matter. We can always print more." Ted continued until he had at least two prints from every negative.

As the papers emerged from the fixing bath, Nelson rinsed them thoroughly in running water, then placed them face down on a cloth to dry.

"Well, are you all set for our trip Monday?" asked Ted, as they were waiting to view the results of their labors.

"I'm all set to have a good time, if that's what you mean," said Nelson, "but you know, the more I think about it, I'm beginning to believe that there never was a gold mine. If there is, why hasn't it been found by now?"

Ted pondered the question. In the rush of the last few weeks he had lost sight of the fact that their only knowledge of the existence of the mine was based on a flood of old rumors plus the photograph which had been found. Yet there had to be a mine, he felt it so strongly, there just had to be.

"If there is a mine, we're going to be the ones to find it," said Ted desperately, "even if we have to stay up there all summer." He walked over to the table where the prints were drying. He overturned the pictures and examined them, and as he did so he gave a startled cry.

"What's the matter?" asked Nelson quickly. "Are some of the pictures spoiled?"

"No, it isn't that," said Ted. "It's this picture here. Look! It—it's a picture of Old Goldie's cabin!"

CHAPTER 13

Back to Thunder Mountain

Nelson ran to Ted's side and peered over his shoulder.

"But that's impossible!" he exclaimed. "How could a picture of Old Goldie's cabin get on my film?"

"It did, though," insisted Ted. From his wallet he withdrew the newspaper clipping he still carried. He unfolded the paper and they compared the pictures. The cabin on Nelson's picture showed the effects of the additional years of weathering, and there were only two pines in front of it, but there could be no doubt that the cabins were the same. There were no windows in front and the door was set a little to the left, while the chimney was on the right, and the background rose in the same manner.

"I don't understand this," said Nelson in a low voice, almost in a whisper. "I don't even remember taking this picture."

"It looks familiar," said Ted, "and still unfamiliar."

Nelson rummaged through his envelope of negatives until he produced the one of the cabin. He examined it carefully through the light, then he exclaimed, "Now I see what happened. Remember that you said you printed some of the pictures with the wrong side of the negative toward the light? This is one of those pictures."

Ted had also made another picture of the cabin which he had printed correctly. They found this print and laid the two pictures side by side. One was the mirror image of the other.

The one that had been printed correctly was a picture of the cabin in which they had spent the night on the mountain. The other showed the cabin of Old Goldie's picture.

"Then that was Old Goldie's cabin where we stayed that night," said Ted. "But it couldn't be. It's on the wrong side of the mountain."

"I think I understand," said Nelson. "When Old Goldie printed his picture he must have reversed the negative. On his picture the shadows all fall to the left, making it appear that the cabin is on the western slope of the mountain. On the real picture the shadows fall to the right, proving that the cabin is actually on the eastern slope."

"That's why no one found the cabin," put in Ted. "Everybody was looking on the wrong side of the mountain." When pictures are reversed in this manner it is often very difficult to recognize the original scene, unless the background is very familiar to you, and the fact that Old Goldie's cabin had aged since the picture was taken added to the difficulty. Most of the searching parties had concentrated on the western slope, and if any of them came across this cabin on the eastern side they did not recognize it.

The boys regarded their discovery in awed silence, hardly grasping the importance of it. They were the ones who had discovered the first clue to the location of Old Goldie's mine. Gone now were all their previous doubts as to the existence of the mine. But they could not help realizing by what a lucky series of happenings they had made their discovery, and the thought filled them with wonder. The sudden shower had driven them into the cabin for shelter, Nelson had decided the cabin made a good photographic study, and Ted, by his ignorance of correct printing procedure, had happened to reverse the negative of that particular picture.

"Still we might have been the ones to find the cabin later in the summer anyway," said Ted, speaking very quietly.

"Yes," agreed Nelson, using the same low tone, "or we might have recognized the cabin from the picture, even if it hadn't been reversed. You came pretty close to recognizing it that morning on the mountain."

For the first time the gold mine was no longer an idle dream but a near reality. Excitedly they formed their plans. They would leave for Thunder Mountain the first thing Monday morning. No questions would be asked of them, for they had already announced their intention of returning to the hills on Monday. There would be no trouble about finding the cabin, but how long it would take them to find the mine they did not know. Anyway, they had supplies for more than a week already packed for their trip.

"In the meantime not a word to anyone," cautioned Nelson, "not even to Ron." Ted had few secrets from Ronald, but he reflected that it would be much more fun to find the mine first and tell Ronald about it afterward.

With their plans completed, and with many additional warnings of secrecy, they separated for the night. The next day Ronald was not his usual cheerful self, and Ted could well sympathize with him. Then he remembered that if all went well Ronald might have the biggest story of his career in time for next Friday's issue. Ronald, for his part, could not help noticing that Ted was in high spirits, but he was accustomed to Ted's ready enthusiasm and attributed it to some vacation project, probably having to do with his baseball team.

It was two grimly determined boys who met at eight o'clock on Monday morning. They rode out to the Breckridge farm almost in silence, leaving their bikes there. After exchanging greetings with the farmer and his wife, they began their long climb up the mountainside. Again the sky was not clear, and it seemed that the weather was about to enter upon another rainy cycle.

"Every time we come to Thunder Mountain it rains," grumbled Nelson.

"Remember that we wouldn't have found the cabin if it hadn't been for the rain," Ted reminded him.

As they drew nearer to the cabin they found themselves growing more tense, for they believed that they were nearing the end of their long quest. When at last they reached the clearing they stopped for a moment to regard the cabin from a distance. Ted drew out the newspaper clipping and they compared the scenes. It was no wonder that they had not recognized the cabin before, for it appeared to be entirely different from the one in the picture. The pine trees, which Nelson had looked for to his right as they ran into the cabin, were really to the left. One of them was down, but as they kicked around in the brush they, uncovered the fallen trunk. They gave a shout of triumph, for to them this was absolute proof that they were on the right track.

"This should be the tree," said Ted, referring to his newspaper clipping once more, then nodding toward one of the pine trees still standing.

"But there's no X carved on the bark," objected Nelson. "Of course not," said Ted. "The X was made on the negative." At least Ronald was right on that point! They looked upward at the tall pine which they somehow felt held the secret of Old Goldie's mine.

"Maybe the entrance to the mine is hidden near the tree. Suppose we tramp about in a circle and see if we can find it," suggested Ted. So they trampled down the underbrush in an ever widening circle, but found nothing to indicate that the mine was close at hand. They returned to the pine tree, discouraged.

"I don't see any arrow or anything else carved on the bark that might show us where the mine is," continued Ted.

"Ron thought it might be like a treasure hunt, with a real treasure at the end." The light laugh which followed helped break the mounting tension. However, there was no symbol carved on the bark. Yet they felt that in this towering plant lay the answer to their problem.

Then Nelson's sharp eyes spied a small hole in the bark about ten feet above the ground. "I wonder if that could be an opening," he muttered, "and if it is—" Ted was quick to grasp the idea, and almost immediately, being lighter than Nelson, he was hoisted onto Nelson's broad shoulders. Prudently he first thrust his pencil into the hole, then felt cautiously about with his fingers.

"Hurray, I have it!" he shouted triumphantly, and then immediately regretted his enthusiasm as Nelson moved and he almost lost his balance. Once more safely on the ground, Ted, breathless, displayed a small metal box. Opening the little container was more than their eager fingers could manage, and Nelson's jackknife was brought into use.

Finally the cover yielded, and Nelson produced a small piece of paper, which, when unfolded, revealed the following: POSFB EWXUW KVWWX WTSSA LW.

"It's in code!" exclaimed Nelson disappointedly.

"But maybe we can break it," said Ted optimistically, adding more doubtfully, "but it's awfully short."

"Maybe you can," said Nelson, for difficult puzzles irritated him. They examined the message carefully. It was printed in large pencil characters, just as were the initials on the envelope and the inscription in the Mother Goose book.

There could little doubt but that it had been written by Old Goldie himself.

Picking up the packs they had thrown on the ground, they hurried into the cabin. Seated at the table with the message spread out before him, Ted took out his notebook and pencil and began his calculations, while Nelson hovered about restlessly. Nelson tried to be of help, but this was not his field. He scratched one ear and then the other. An onlooker might have thought that he did his thinking with his ears.

"Why don't you take the most common letter and call it E?" he asked helpfully. "I've heard that's the way to start breaking a code message."

"That's just what I have been doing," said Ted, giving him a grim look, "but I don't seem to be getting anywhere. The message is really too short to be broken very easily." He continued to work at the code for half an hour, but finally he gave it up.

"I don't think I can do anything with it," he said. "Nothing is coming out. I have a feeling that this code isn't a very simple one, that some hard kind of system has been used. It doesn't look like the kind of code where one letter is substituted for another."

"What other kinds of codes do you know?" asked Nelson. Ted's knowledge of codes was almost as limited as was Nelson's, and although he had a few ideas on the subject, he could hardly do more than speculate.

"There's six W's," said Nelson. "Maybe that means something."

"Maybe it does," returned Ted, smiling a little in spite of himself.

"But if we can't read the code message," said Nelson, "I don't see that we are any better off than we were before."

"Oh, I think we are. At least we know this is Old Goldie's cabin, which is more than anyone else knows, and we are the only ones to know about the code message. But I am very much afraid that if we have to depend on this code message to find Old Goldie's mine, we aren't going to find it."

CHAPTER 14

Mr. Gumber

The picture which Ted had of Old Goldie had been gradually chang-ing. He had always thought of the man as being an uneducated, rather simple-minded old prospector who spent his time wandering about through the hills, probably for lack of anything better to occupy himself. But now the prospector had not only tricked them all by reversing the picture of his cabin, but he had also left a code message which was too difficult for them to break.

"That old prospector was a regular fox," said Nelson. "People have been looking for his mine for years and never found it. It must be very well hidden."

"I can't help but feel that there is more purpose to this affair than we realize," said Ted. "If Old Goldie didn't want anyone to find his mine, why did he leave the picture and the message? Yet if he did want some-one to find it, why did he reverse the picture and write the message using a difficult code?"

"It must be that the message was meant for a certain person," rea-soned Nelson. "It must be that man T.A.F. The envelope was meant for him, so probably the code message was meant for him, too. If we could find T.A.F., I believe he could read this message, find the mine, and ex-plain the whole mystery."

Ted had been filled with the idea that little Tim was T.A.F., but now he had to consider seriously that T.A.F. might be someone else.

"Still, why didn't T.A.F. come forward and claim the envelope?" asked Nelson.

"There was no reason why he should," said Ted. "After the picture had been printed in the papers, it became public knowledge. He had nothing further to gain by claiming the envelope Perhaps he thought he would have a better chance of searching for the mine if no one else knew about him."

"Sometimes I wonder," said Nelson, "if there really is a gold mine after all. All this, the picture, the cabin, and the code message might have an entirely different meaning." He did not really believe this, but merely offered it as a possibility. They wanted to believe there was a gold mine, and they would continue to believe it until all the evidence pointed to the contrary.

There was silence for a few moments. They had thought that once the cabin was found finding the mine would be easy, but all the cabin had given them was the code message, a clue they could not use. They were each debating the same question—the problem of what to do next.

"I wish Ron were here," said Ted. "Maybe he could help us."

"But if he knew about this cabin he would print it in the paper," objected Nelson. "Then we would have the whole town up here."

"If Ron had found the cabin himself he might have felt obliged to put it in the paper," said Ted, "but if we told him about it it would be our secret, and he would keep it."

As a matter of fact the boys both felt the need of an older person's advice. With the knowledge that they had actually found Old Goldie's cabin had come the realization that they were facing a problem which loomed too big for them. Ronald, especially, would be an ideal person to share their secret, for he was only a few years older than they, and in addition probably knew more about the case than anyone else. On the other hand, now that they were so close to their goal, they were reluctant to leave the scene.

"We can't leave here now and take a chance on someone else's discovering the mine," asserted Nelson. A compromise readily suggested itself. Ted would go for Ronald, while Nelson would remain at the cabin, meanwhile beginning the search for the mine. Prudently Ted first made another copy of the code message, which he gave to Nelson, taking the original copy with him.

After a quick lunch he started out, promising to be back before evening. The trip down the mountain took hardly more than an hour, but he did not arrive as soon as he had hoped. From his wristwatch he ascertained that he had already missed the one o'clock bus into town. He was about to turn in at the Breckridge farm for his bicycle when a car pulled up at the side of the road, and Mr. Aimsley, a former neighbor of the Wilford family, invited him to hop in. Ted gladly accepted the invitation, for not only would he make better time, but he was glad of the opportunity to renew his acquaintance with Mr. Aimsley, who no longer lived in town.

Naturally Mr. Aimsley teased Ted about Old Goldie's mine, for why else had Ted gone to Thunder Mountain?

"But weren't you on the wrong side of the mountain?" he asked.

"It's closer to climb this side and cross over through the pass than to go around by road," explained Ted, truthfully enough, and changed the subject as soon as possible. They chatted together, and Ted recalled a time when Ronald had shouted, "Fire!" so earnestly that the family believed him, only to discover that it was an April fool joke. Mr. Aimsley had repaid Ronald, though, by giving him a cold shower "to put out the fire."

"I have sometimes thought that perhaps we were a little too severe with Ronald," said Mr. Aimsley.

"I hardly think so," Ted answered. "He hasn't played any more April fool jokes since then."

At this moment the object of their conversation was engaged in an unusual mission of his own. Returning to his office after lunch, Ronald had been told that a Mr. Gumber, a mining engineer, had called that morning and requested an interview with him at the hotel. Mystified by the request, Ronald nevertheless went to the hotel immediately and asked for Mr. Gumber at the desk. Being advised that Mr. Gumber would see him in Room 212, he went upstairs.

Mr. Gumber answered his knock, introduced himself, and invited him to sit down. "I suppose you are wondering why I asked to see you, Mr. Wilford. I am a mining engineer by profession, and in fact I was one of the engineers who made a survey of this region a number of years ago. You may remember the occasion. At the time there were widespread rumors concerning a gold mine which the prospector, Old Goldie, was supposed to have.

"Naturally I have been much interested in the way the story has recently been revived, especially so since the survey I made showed no signs of gold in this vicinity. I thought that I would get in touch with you, in view of the fact that you were the one who broke the story, scoring quite a scoop with it, I understand. I wonder if you would mind telling me, Mr. Wilford, if you have any definite facts to indicate that there really is a gold mine located in this district."

Ronald, as it happened, had very few facts to go on beyond what he had stated in his newspaper articles, except for a few speculations of his own on which he did not care to dwell. Nevertheless he was glad to have the opportunity to discus the case with an expert in the mining field.

"I am afraid that those rumors really do form the basis for the story," he said, "although there are a few other facts which are difficult to explain except on the assumption that there is a gold mine. There is, of course, the picture which was found; also various details in Old Goldie's past life lead to a belief in the existence of the mine."

They went on to discuss the case, Mr. Gumber asking many questions on details which Ronald had not fully explained in his stories. Ronald, on his part, had a few questions of his own to ask. He was especially interested in knowing if there was anything in his theory that the mine would not be located near a stream.

"There is something in the idea," agreed the engineer cautiously, "but it would depend on a great many circumstances, such as the character of the soil, the level of the water table, the force of the running water, the amount of rainfall, and so on. Tests which were made on the streams, while they are helpful in tracking down the location of gold deposits if gold is shown, do not necessarily eliminate the possibility of gold in a district if the results of the test are negative."

The discussion drew to a close a little later, and Ronald rose to go, feeling that his time had been profitably spent. Mr. Gumber went downstairs with him.

"I suppose you are going to look for the mine like everyone else," said Ronald with a smile.

"I may go up into the mountains for a few days," admitted the engineer. "The problem is an interesting one. Quite frankly I do have another motive. I am working more or less independently at this time, and regardless of who finds the mine, I would welcome the job of managing and developing it."

Ronald was much surprised to find Ted waiting for him as he and Mr. Gumber entered the reception room. Ted was bursting with his news, but he waited patiently until the necessary introduction was performed. Then by a slight raising of his eyes he asked whether it was all right to speak in front of Mr. Gumber, and by an almost imperceptible nod Ronald indicated that it was.

"Mr. Gumber is a mining engineer, and once made a survey of this region," said Ronald by way of explanation. "We have just had a very interesting discussion."

Mr. Gumber noted Ted's hesitation, and said quickly, "If it's anything to do with Old Goldie's mine, your brother and I have been very frank with each other, and I think he will tell you that I can be counted upon for secrecy."

Ted turned to observe his new acquaintance. He was of average height, broad-shouldered, and somewhat overweight. Although he appeared to be about thirty-five, a certain bitterness had crept into his features which was out of keeping with his years. Yet the point which struck Ted most forcibly was that Mr. Gumber's face seemed strangely familiar. Altogether, although he did not often make snap judgments of people, Ted's first impression of Mr. Gumber was a favorable one.

"Well, then," said Ted dramatically, "we found Old Goldie's cabin!"

The young reporter whistled his surprise. "Was it about where I said it would be?" he asked.

On only a few occasions during his life had Ted ever had the opportunity to astonish his brother, and even more seldom was he able to prove Ronald wrong on any important subject, so today he took full advantage of the situation.

"No," he replied, "it was on the opposite side of the mountain," and he went on to explain how the photograph had been reversed.

"It took a smart lad to figure that out," said Mr. Gumber. Ordinarily Ted was suspicious of flattery, but the words of praise from the engineer had a ring of sincerity, and he made a modest rejoinder. Ronald stood silent for a moment, contemplating the turn events had taken, and finally he laughed.

"I don't know what Crusty will say when he finds out I had the whole town searching on the wrong side of the mountain." Then he added, "But if the cabin is where you say, at least I was partly right. That would be just about halfway between Forestdale and North Ridge, only on the eastern slope instead of the western. But are you sure this is the right cabin, Ted?"

"If you need any proof here it is," and from his pocket Ted produced his copy of the secret message.

"A code message!" exclaimed Mr. Gumber, and he appeared to be much interested. "Where did you get this?" Ted explained how the message had been found.

"So that's what the X on the pine tree meant," said Ronald. "Hm, did you try to break the code?"

"Yes, but I couldn't." For the first time Ted had the opportunity to explain to Ronald the plan they had made— that Ronald would come back to the cabin with Ted and help search for the mine—and Ronald was not only willing but enthusiastic. His assignments had slackened off, and he had no more important story than this one. He felt that he could easily afford to spend a day or two in the quest.

"How would it be if I were to come along?" asked Mr. Gumber. "This problem interests me, and possibly I can be of help."

"Glad to have you," said Ronald. "A mining expert may be just what we need."

While speaking he thrust the message into the pocket of his topcoat. As Mr. Gumber walked across the room to make arrangements with the desk clerk, Ted was struck once more by the engineer's resemblance to someone whom he knew but could not place.

CHAPTER 15

A Midnight Alarm

"Mr. Gumber was interested in my story because of the survey be once made, and asked for an interview," Ronald explained to Ted. "I hope you don't object to my inviting him along. He's very definitely a first-class mining engineer, and would like the job of developing the mine for us if we should find it."

"No," said Ted slowly, "no, he might be of help to us. Besides, I rather like him. He seems a very friendly sort of person."

"That's about the way I had him sized up," agreed Ronald, "friendly, but reserved." They had time to say nothing more, for Mr. Gumber rejoined them just then. It was quickly agreed that the trip to the Breckridge farm would be made in Jeremiah.

Several stops had to be made first: Ronald reported back to his office, additional supplies were purchased, and they stopped at the Wilford home to inform Mrs. Wilford that Ronald, too, would be absent at least for the night. The diminutive lady wished them luck and asked no questions, although she must have guessed very closely to the truth.

Ronald changed into sports clothes, as being more suitable to the occasion. The topcoat he had worn during the day was thrown into the back seat, and once more they were on their way.

"I wonder if there is any chance we can break that code message," said Ronald when they were on the highway headed toward the mountain.

"I don't think we can," put in Ted. "The message is so short. I tried that method of finding the letter that is used the most and calling it E, but it didn't work out."

"That method wouldn't work," said Mr. Gumber, "unless it is a simple letter substitution type code. It is quite possible that a more difficult system was employed."

"Still," said Ronald, "you would hardly expect a person like Old Goldie to use a difficult code system."

"There are thousands of different code systems," said Mr. Gumber, "and a good many of them are easy to use but difficult for outsiders to break."

"You don't happen to be a code expert as well as a mining engineer, do you?" asked Ronald with a laugh.

"Afraid not," returned Mr. Gumber, "though I wish I were."

Ronald proceeded, "I have heard of another kind of code, where a message is written by referring to letters or words in a book." Ted knew that Ronald was thinking of the Mother Goose book.

"Yes, there are codes like that," agreed Mr. Gumber. "One method is to combine the letters of the message with the letters in the book, using a prearranged formula for combining letters. But if the code is anything like that, I'm certain we won't be able to break it. Even experts have trouble breaking codes of that type."

"This whole affair is becoming more strange," mused Ronald. "No one would expect Old Goldie to reverse that photograph, and then to leave a code message in a pine tree."

"There's no accounting for some of the things those old prospectors do," said Mr. Gumber. "They sometimes get kind of queer, being by themselves so much of the time."

During the rest of the ride Mr. Gumber told the boys something of his work, and he left no doubt in their minds that he was a mining expert of the most competent sort. He explained an instrument for locating mineral deposits by bombarding the earth with electrons, and Ted and Ronald, always interested in scientific developments, listened attentively.

"Something like an old-fashioned divining rod, only a lot more scientific," Mr. Gumber concluded. Ronald turned the car in at the Breckridge farm, and the genial farmer, working in a field near by, motioned them on into the barn, and came over to speak with them.

"Still hunting for that gold mine, I reckon," he declared, "We've seen a lot of parties go up the mountain these last weeks, though mostly they drove around the mountain and went up the other side. Maybe you fellows know something the rest of us don't."

"Might be," laughed Ronald noncommittally, realizing that it was useless to pretend to be on any other mission. "We'll probably stop back for the car some time tomorrow or the next day."

Their supplies having been bundled up so that they could be carried easily, the trio began the long climb up the trail. Their progress was slower than they had expected, for Ted was more tired than when he made the trip earlier in the day, and Ronald and Mr. Gumber soon discovered that they were not in first-class condition for mountain climbing.

It was getting on toward evening when the old cabin was reached. Nelson had eagerly awaited the arrival of the party. His own afternoon had been spent in getting their supplies in order for a long stay, and he had done some more searching for the mine in the near neighborhood, but without result. He further reported that he had seen no one on the mountain during the afternoon. He was introduced to Mr. Gumber, took an immediate liking to him, and was glad he had been added to the party.

Eager as they were to begin the search, they realized that they could hope to accomplish little that day. Nevertheless they did search for about an hour, in a more or less haphazard fashion, hoping that they might stumble upon the mine by accident. Their systematic search would take place the next day. They sat down to a late supper, consisting chiefly of baked beans, that staple food which invariably graces every masculine table.

It was dark when they finished, and most of the members of the party would have been content to relax, but not the lively Nelson. He expressed a desire to see the sunset.

"The sunset?" said Ted with a yawn. "I thought the sun went down long ago." Nelson reminded his companion that they were on the eastern slope of the mountain, and that by traveling farther up the trail to a point overlooking the pass the spectacle could still be observed in all its radiant glory.

But Ted, who had walked much farther than any of the others that day, was uninterested in the beauties of nature, and stated his intention of taking a short nap upon the bunk; Mr. Gumber also found no special favor in the idea.

Ronald was also tired, but it had been several years since he had been able to hike on Thunder Mountain as he pleased, and he allowed himself to be persuaded by Nelson's urging.

"The clouds were dandy today," said Nelson, "so the sunset should be a good one." So Ronald and Nelson made the little trip alone through the dusk. They were friends of long standing, and the few years' difference in their ages no longer seemed important. Ronald occasionally allowed himself to be beaten at table tennis by Nelson who was an expert player, and Nelson, for his part, never tired of listening to Ronald's tales of his newspaper experiences.

The trail which they followed wound upward, but was not very steep. About half a mile away was the spring which spouted forth from the mountainside, forming the beginning of the mountain stream. They picked their way across the stream, and less than half a mile beyond the trail took a sharp turn to the west, where, by standing on a jutting bluff, they were afforded a view of the western sky.

Nelson's promise had not been an idle one. The clouds which had dotted the sky earlier in the day had not disappeared, and now served to reflect the dying beams in a blaze of color. As the sky faded into a deep gray Nelson's attention was diverted elsewhere. His sharp eyes noticed a wisp of smoke coming from a cabin far below them on the other side of the pass. He called it to Ronald's attention.

"I guess we have some neighbors," murmured Ronald. "That's the cabin where we found the Mother Goose book!" exclaimed Nelson.

"Whoever it was is still there." Ronald was more disturbed by the news than he cared to show. "There have been a lot of parties on the mountain," he said doubtfully. "It might not even be the same person."

"I would like to know who it is, though," said Nelson, "and how he came to have the Mother Goose book. Don't you think we ought to go down there and find out? Maybe it would solve the whole case."

"I don't think so," returned Ronald, "not just at this time. Remember our immediate objective is to find the gold mine, and the next point is to learn what we can about Old Goldie and the rest of the case. Whoever the person is, even if he is the one who brought the Mother Goose book here, he probably doesn't know yet about Old Goldie's cabin or the code message. Our job is cut out for us, and that is to find the mine."

Nevertheless, the presence of another person in the cabin at Moosehead Pass troubled them vaguely, and it was with a feeling of uneasiness that they walked back toward their cabin. With the fall of night a slight chill sprang up, and they made the return trip as rapidly as possible until once more they found themselves in the cozy room of the cabin. They sat about the fire discussing the case once more from every angle. Then the talk drifted into more general lines.

"I remember the time I was caught in a cave-in in a coal mine," began Mr. Gumber, and went on to relate how a section of the timbers had crossed to hold back the slide and form a pocket, how an air tube was pushed down to them when the air was almost exhausted, how later supplies were sent down and they were finally rescued after two days beneath the earth.

The others, too, had interesting experiences to contribute. Mr. Gumber had lost the air of distraction he sometimes carried, and for a time at least was one of them. The lines of his face and the puckering of his brow had lessened, and he appeared much younger than he did before.

People who live close to nature generally regulate their living to conform more nearly to the rising and setting of the sun than do town folk, and that night it was commonly agreed that a policy of early to bed and early to rise would be a wise one. They expected the coming day to be an important one for them, and wanted to be as fresh as possible for their search. To Mr. Gumber went the dubious privilege of occupying the bunk, and his objections were finally overruled. Ronald declared that he would roll himself up in a blanket before the fire.

"I never did get over that cold shower I had," he said with a laugh, knowing that Nelson had heard the story.

As for Ted and Nelson, they had other plans for themselves. The loft in the cabin was as yet unexplored, and they expressed their intention of passing the night within its shadows. First every corner had to be searched, amid whoops and shouts, but quiet soon settled over the cabin more suddenly than one would have believed possible. They were all more tired than they realized following the rather unusual exertion of the day. The cool mountain air, too, hastened their drift into their separate slumberlands. The rain returned a little later, and the gentle patter on the roof served as a lullaby. Somewhere an owl hooted in the distance. Within the cabin the fire died down until the fireplace was filled with the red glow of dying embers.

No more peaceful scene could be imagined, so it was surprising that about an hour after midnight Ronald should have been aroused into half consciousness by a slight noise, which he later declared might have been the creak of a floor board or the lowering of the window. He was startled into full wakefulness a moment later by an outcry from Mr. Gumber: "Look out! I saw a face at the window—the face of an Indian!"

CHAPTER 16

The Search Continues

At the sudden alarm everyone immediately became active. Ted and Nelson streamed down the ladder partly dressed, while Ronald slipped into his shoes, caught up a flashlight and his coat which was hanging on a nail near the window, and dashed outside. He remained there for ten minutes, walking about the cabin several times, and on one occasion following one of the trails for a short distance. Then he reentered the cabin with a discouraged air.

"There's no sign of him," he said. "Are you sure it was an Indian?"

"Undoubtedly," said Mr. Gumber. "His face was pressed rather closely against the window, and I could see the prominent cheekbones and the black hair." Ted and Nelson had already made up their minds about the matter.

"Jim Rivers!" they exclaimed together. Mr. Gumber had heard the story of Jim Rivers.

"It might be," he affirmed. Ted recalled how he believed they had been followed by Jim Rivers after they left the cabin at Moosehead Pass. "Jim must be looking for the mine, too. Perhaps he's using that cabin where you saw the smoke."

"So Jim Rivers is here on the mountain," muttered Ronald. Idly he thrust his hand into the pocket of the coat he was still wearing. Then he exclaimed, "Say, my copy of the code message is gone!" Gone! They all looked at each other, startled. "I'm sure I put it in this pocket," continued Ronald.

Ted was able to confirm this, for he remembered how Ronald had placed the paper in his pocket as they stood in the reception room at the hotel. "Could it have fallen out?" asked Ted anxiously.

"Not very easily. The pocket is a deep one, and it has a flap." Ronald looked about tragically.

"That Indian, Jim Rivers!" exclaimed Nelson suddenly. "Your coat was hanging right by the window. Couldn't he have opened the window, reached in and got the message, and closed the window again."

Ronald, remembering the slight noise he had heard Just before Mr. Gumber's outcry, stated reflectively, "He might have, provided he had any idea that the message was in my pocket." A hasty check revealed that the window, in spite of its age, opened quite easily and almost without noise. Perhaps the sound which first awakened Ronald was the gentle closing of the window.

"For that matter," said Mr. Gumber, "I have no doubt that an Indian could actually have entered the cabin and searched it without awakening any of us. They are rather a stealthy lot, trained to walk silently through the woods tracking game and things like that."

"Or he might have seen the coat from the window and made a lucky guess," opined Nelson. Whatever the explanation, Ronald's copy of the code message was gone. "But we still have the other copy to work with," Ted declared hopefully. Their hearts fluttered for a moment, but a quick look revealed that Nelson's copy was still safe in his billfold.

"But why should Jim steal the message?" asked Ted. "He won't be able to read it any better than we can—unless he is T.A.F." Since Jim's initials were obviously not T.A.F., this latter possibility was dismissed.

"Perhaps Jim didn't know the message was in code," suggested Nelson.

Ronald also had another possible solution. "It might be that Jim already knows where the mine is, and he stole the message because he was afraid we might be able to read the code and discover the mine. He didn't know that we had another copy of the message."

It was probable that one of these explanations was the correct one, though which one they could not tell. There was nothing further to be done, and after agreeing that Jim was not likely to return that night they drifted back to their sleeping quarters. In spite of the excitement everyone fell asleep, but it was not as deep a sleep as before, and the slightest noise aroused them back into wakefulness.

Everyone was up almost with the sun the next morning. The alarm of the night was discussed once more, but in the bright summer light it seemed strange and impossible, as though it could not have happened. That an Indian had lurked about in the shadows, watching their moves and waiting for a chance to steal the message, must have been part of a dream.

Ronald wandered through the cabin and then outside, jotting down notes for the newspaper story he intended to write as soon as the boys would release him from his promise of secrecy. Mr. Gumber volunteered to prepare breakfast, a task at which Ronald later assisted. Before long Ted and Nelson returned from an invigorating dip in the mountain stream, and they all sat down to a meal of crisp bacon and potatoes.

"Don't you think we ought to go over to that other cabin and see about Jim Rivers?" suggested Nelson.

Again Ronald opposed the idea. "Our job is to find the mine," he maintained. Their plans for the day were discussed, and it was agreed that they would split into two parties, Ronald and Mr. Gumber to explore the territory to the north, which the engineer believed to be more promising, while Ted and Nelson would explore to the south.

Mr. Gumber could offer them but little advice. "If this were an ordinary prospecting trip I could tell you what signs to be on the watch for, but all the hills have already been well prospected, and I doubt that any of the usual signs will be present. Besides, this situation is different. Our problem is to find a mine that has already been worked, and that probably has been deliberately concealed in some manner. The mine might be a natural cave, the entrance to which has been hidden or blocked off. Be on the lookout for any signs that man has disturbed the handiwork of nature."

Ted and Nelson, who knew Ronald well, could not help noticing that he was not as boisterous as usual. He appeared to be very thoughtful, and did not speak much unless someone addressed him first. Now, however, he made a suggestion.

"All we really have to go on is this cabin," he said. "It would seem reasonable to me that Old Goldie would have built his cabin somewhere near his mine. This would make it easy for him to reach it and work it while he lived here. I would suggest that we use this cabin as a starting point, and confine our search to within a mile of the cabin."

As no better idea presented itself, the others agreed. Ted thought he detected an undercurrent to Ronald's words, and believed he could guess its meaning. Although not wishing to alarm the others, Ronald was not easy in his own mind about the parties separating, particularly as Nelson and Ted were to have the territory toward the other cabin, and hoped that they would remain in sight of each other most of the day.

Although they did not expect to be gone far from the cabin, lunches were packed so that it would not be necessary to reassemble at noon, and they all headed up the mountainside together. At a point about half a mile beyond the cabin they separated, Ronald and Mr. Gumber turning toward the north, leaving the two boys to take the southern section, with admonitions from both sides that the others should be sure to return to the cabin before six o'clock.

Ronald was still thoughtful. He carried on the search carefully, but he did not attempt to engage the engineer in conversation. Mr. Gumber lingered from time to time to pick up rock specimens and examine them carefully, but each time he would shake his head and toss them down again, and they would push on.

The territory assigned to Ted and Nelson was more open than most of the surrounding slope. This, they hoped, would make their search easier.

"It seems to me that if I were going to conceal the entrance to a mine I would roll a boulder in front of it," declared Ted, and so they carefully searched behind boulders which Nelson asserted were too big for ten men to move. Ted explained that by the use of engineering principles it is possible for a man to move objects considerably heavier than himself.

"I know this much," asserted Nelson, "Old Goldie didn't take one of these big boulders and push it aside every time he wanted to reach his mine."

"But we don't know that he did visit the mine recently," argued Ted. "The mine may have been blocked off for years."

"Didn't you think Ron was kind of quiet this morning?" asked Nelson a little later.

"Yes," agreed Ted, "I think he was worrying about that Indian." But the boys were not worried about Jim Rivers in broad daylight, and perhaps would have welcomed a meeting with him. It was impossible on that rugged hillside for the two parties to remain in sight of each other all day, for jutting ridges and numerous trees often cut off their view. But they did see each other on many occasions, and sometimes were within hailing distance, though they did not get close enough to talk.

For hours they trampled the underbrush and explored rocky crevices, but without finding any trace of the mine. Every slight depression was an object of suspicion; every unusual mound might be a pile of dirt used to fill up an old hole; every bush or rock might conceal the entrance to a cave; every tree might be a landmark serving as a guide to the location of the mine.

The day was cool, and the skies remained threatening. Ted and Nelson carried their search as far as the spring. Then they zigzagged up and down the slope, sometimes as far down as the original trail they had followed to Moosehead Pass, searching as carefully and as thoroughly as they could. Nowhere did they find any indication that the character of the hillside had been disturbed by man.

At noon they stopped to rest and to eat lunch. "I wonder if the others have found anything," Nelson speculated, nibbling on a sandwich.

"I hardly think so," said Ted, "or they would have hailed us before now." Mr. Gumber and Ronald were out of sight at the time.

"Then that must mean that the mine is very well hidden," said Nelson, "or else we're on the wrong track altogether."

After lunch they took up the search again, up and down the mountain, and although they found nothing, they at least had the satisfaction, as the afternoon waned, of feeling they had covered their territory thoroughly.

"I feel sure the mine isn't anywhere in the part we searched," said Nelson. Ted was not so certain, but nevertheless felt inclined to agree. They returned to the cabin somewhat after five. It was still early, and the older members of the party were not in sight. Expecting them soon, the boys began to prepare supper.

Ronald returned alone a little later, looking serious. "Listen. Mr. Gumber is still down the trail. I have something I want to tell you before he gets back."

CHAPTER 17

Suspicions

Ronald spoke slowly at first, not certain that he could make his point clear.

"I wanted to warn you fellows. I have an idea that Mr. Gumber isn't just what he claims to be." Ted and Nelson regarded him in surprise.

"But Ron, he is a mining engineer, isn't he?" asked Ted. "Oh, he's a mining expert, all right," replied Ronald.

"We've been practically bombarding him with questions, and he comes through each barrage with flying colors. I don't think he could very well deceive us on that point. But just what he is up to I don't know." They waited for him to explain his suspicions. "The more I think about what happened last night the less I am able to understand it. Do you realize that no one saw that Indian except Mr. Gumber?"

"You mean that he only imagined he saw an Indian?" asked Ted.

"I don't mean it in quite that way. Mr. Gumber isn't the imaginative type. I mean that he deliberately created an Indian for our imaginations to conceal his own theft of the code message!"

They stood stunned by this sudden pronouncement. Then Ted found breath to say, "Ron, that's impossible."

"Is it? Then what else are we supposed to believe? That Jim Rivers followed you boys on the trail yesterday morning and saw you discover the code message, that he waited about for an opportunity to steal the message, and that he later managed to steal it by reaching in through the window, although he could not possibly have known in advance that it was in my coat pocket? Mr. Gumber was a little too ready with his explanation of how Jim might actually have entered the cabin and searched it, a situation that seems impossible to me. Then again, the ground was soft in many spots, and yet I could find no trace of footprints."

"Then you believe that Mr. Gumber actually took the message?"

Ronald said firmly, "I'm not stating it as a positive fact, but it appears likely to me that there never was an Indian at that window, and that the code message now rests snugly in Mr. Gumber's pocket. He knew that Old Goldie once had an Indian guide, that an Indian had been seen in town—I remember we discussed that point at our interview—and that we had seen smoke coming from the other cabin. He may have realized how easily he could lead us to believe that the message was stolen by an Indian."

Ted shook his head doubtfully. "It's hard to believe Jim Rivers stole the message, but remember you may have lost it, and maybe Mr. Gumber really did see Jim at the window."

Ronald looked out the window. Mr. Gumber was still examining rocks down the trail. "There is something else. This morning when I came into the cabin I got the impression that Mr. Gumber had Just thrown something into the fire. Later I put out the fire, and I found this." He held out a scrap of paper, partly burned, on which they could make out the following:

W 322 X 323 Y 331 Q 232 Z 332 I 133 R 233 & 333.

"What do you think of this?" asked Ronald.

"Why—it looks like some kind of code," exclaimed Ted, while Nelson looked on with close interest.

"That's just what I thought, too."

"Ronald, if this really was used to break the code message, there ought to be some way we can figure it out, too."

"I don't know," said Ronald doubtfully. "The message is so short, and we have only a small scrap of this paper, whatever it might be—and I ought to remind you that it might be something entirely different. But it does look like code. I don't know much about codes myself, bat perhaps an expert could do something with it."

"Not now!" objected Nelson. "We can't let anyone else know where the mine is. They might jump in and claim it ahead of us. You weren't going to print anything about it, were you?"

"Of course not. This was your secret, and I'm pledged to silence until the mine is found and claimed, or until you release me. I only wish I were certain Mr. Gumber could be relied on to keep his pledge, too."

Ted said slowly, "Then you think that Mr. Gumber is a code expert, and that he stole the code message because he thought he would be able to break it?"

"Something like that," admitted Ronald. "But Ron, if Mr. Gumber has read the code message, perhaps he already knows where the mine is."

"Oh, I doubt that he knows where the mine is yet," said Ronald. "Even if he is an expert it would take him some time to break the message. I don't believe he has had time for that so far."

Ted had listened to Ronald's opinions, but now his sense of loyalty came surging to the fore. It was not merely that he was accustomed to think the best of people, but also that he had actually grown to like Mr. Gumber. The way he had told of his mining experiences, his easygoing but intelligent answers to their queries, the matter-of-fact way in which he addressed Ted by his nickname and dropped into the habit of calling Ronald by his first name—surely these were not the earmarks of a thief.

"Ron, I can't believe that Mr. Gumber stole the message and is trying to cheat us out of the mine. I can't explain it, but for some reason I like Mr. Gumber and trust him."

"That's strange," said Ronald, "because I feel the same way about him myself, or I certainly would never have invited him to come with us."

They had time to say nothing more, for Just then Mr. Gumber started up the path toward the cabin. Ronald hastily stuffed his notebook and the scrap of paper back into his pocket. When Mr. Gumber rejoined them, Ted was forced to admit that there was something decidedly reserved about the engineer's manner. Perhaps Ronald was right, for Mr. Gumber could easily have taken the message. He had seen Ronald place it in his pocket, and had invited himself along on the expedition. And it was true that no one else had seen the Indian. How confused everything was getting!

Supper was a quiet meal that evening. Each of the members of the party was filled with his own thoughts. Ronald was blaming himself for having invited a doubtful person to accompany them to the mountain, and to share their secret, thus endangering the success of the boys' plans.

Ted, still trying to make up his mind about Mr. Gumber, was weighing all the evidence against him, but was still undecided. Nelson was a forthright person, and, if left to his own devices, would probably have confronted Mr. Gumber with the facts against him and demanded an explanation. But Ronald showed no sign of doing this, so Nelson did not act upon the idea on his own initiative.

As for Mr. Gumber, perhaps he attributed the dejected atmosphere to disappointment over their failure to find the mine that day, and he tried to cast a cheerful light on things.

"Never mind. You have a better start toward finding the mine than anyone else has, and you still have all summer to look for it."

"They have all summer," corrected Ronald, "but I'm afraid that I have wasted all the time here I can afford to. My deadline is Thursday morning, and I have a number of things to do before then. I believe I shall have to desert the expedition this evening."

It is certain that Ronald, with his present suspicions of the engineer, would not have left the boys alone with him under any circumstances, deadline or no. However, the engineer fell in with his plan.

"Yes," said Mr. Gumber, "and I believe I had better be getting back, too. I have several business matters to attend to, and it appears that my mining experience isn't going to be of much help in finding the mine."

Ted and Nelson were much surprised at the sudden manner in which their party had begun to disintegrate. They had thought that, as long as the mine had not been found, the party would stay together at least until the next day. However, Ted, at least, must have realized that Ronald's object was to get Mr. Gumber away from the cabin, so he did not urge Ronald to change his mind.

"If we are going tonight," said Ronald, "we had better leave soon. There's only an hour or so of daylight left, and we want to get down to the farm before dark."

"Yes," agreed Mr. Gumber, rising from the table, "we had better be on our way."

The others finished their meal as quickly as possible, clearing up afterward. It was decided that most of the supplies Ronald had brought with him would be left there, but he and Mr. Gumber both had some personal effects which they set about gathering up to take with them.

"We'll stay here as long as our supplies hold out," Ted told Ronald in a low voice while Mr. Gumber was on the other side of the room.

"All right," said Ronald, "and I may possibly come back in a few days, if I can get away. I have a lot of things I want to check into, though, first. And Ted," he glanced over toward Mr. Gumber as he spoke, "take good care of yourself."

Ted was surprised at the seriousness of Ronald's remark. He wished that he could have a chance to discuss a few matters with Ronald before he left, but it was not possible under the circumstances. Perhaps Ronald spoke more seriously than he intended. With the solicitude of an older brother, he had not yet accustomed himself to the fact that Ted was growing up, and was capable of taking care of himself. Just what danger threatened the boys alone in the cabin he did not know. For even if Mr. Gumber was guilty of the things of which they suspected him, that danger would disappear when he left the mountain. Even that danger was only a very tentative one, for regardless of what Mr. Gumber's intentions might be toward the mine, he was quite sure the engineer would never inflict any injury upon them in any other respect.

In spite of himself he discovered that he still liked Mr. Gumber, regardless of the suspicious circumstances which surrounded his entrance into the case and his subsequent actions. As to the other possible source of danger—that of the Indian they supposed was on the mountain—Ronald had just about made up his mind that the Indian was only a myth, in which Mr. Gumber had cleverly led them to believe.

As they were ready to leave, Mr. Gumber said, "I'm sorry I wasn't able to be of more help to you. If you should find the mine, you might get in touch with me. I might be able to help in its development."

"I guess they'll have to find it first," said Ronald. He thrust his hand into his coat pocket and stopped speaking abruptly as a look of surprise spread over his face. He felt about for a moment, probing deeply, and when he withdrew his hand there was a small slip of paper in it—the code message!

CHAPTER 18

Ronald Wonders

They all looked at the piece of paper in surprise "The code message!" exclaimed Ted. "But how did it get in your pocket?"

"It must have been there all the time," explained Ronald. "There is a small tear in the lining at the top of the pocket. I didn't know it was there. The paper must have slipped down there when I first put it in my pocket. I remember that I never took it out since then."

Ted and Nelson were especially surprised at the unexpected turn of events. When Ronald had outlined his suspicions to them, they had not wanted to believe him, but they had to admit that the evidence against Mr. Gumber was grave. But that evidence had disappeared, for he could hardly have stolen the code message if it had never left Ronald's pocket. The atmosphere in the cabin immediately became more cheerful, now that the veil of doubt had been lifted.

Mr. Gumber alone showed no special surprise at the discovery. "I remember something like that happened to me when I was a boy," he said. "I lost a dime that way, and I didn't find it until weeks after. A dime meant a lot to me in those days, too."

The two boys were ashamed of themselves. How could they ever have suspected Mr. Gumber of any unorthodox actions? With his recollection of the lost dime he had completely disarmed all their suspicions.

"I suppose we may as well be leaving," said Ronald, somewhat doubtfully. His immediate reason for leaving the mountain had disappeared, but there seemed no way in which he could change his plan without explaining his former suspicions to the engineer.

"Yes, it's beginning to grow dark," said Mr. Gumber. They got their things together, and a few minutes later left the cabin and started down the trail. Ronald was still not easy in his mind about leaving the boys alone. If Mr. Gumber was correct about the Indian he had seen in the window, then that danger still presented itself. Ron did not believe that Jim Rivers—if it was he—would hurt the boys, but it was not a comfortable feeling to know that they were being closely spied upon, with all their movements watched. But he knew Ted was a careful, level-headed boy, and over and over again told himself that Ted and Nelson were old enough to watch out for themselves.

Other doubts persisted in Ronald's mind. He had to admit to himself that he was not entirely satisfied with the way in which the code message had reappeared so opportunely. It is quite possible, he told himself, for a person to have a hole in his pocket he knows nothing about, and the explanation he had made about the code message slipping down in to the lining was a plausible one.

But there was another possible explanation to the affair. Gumber could have taken the message, copied it, and torn a small hole in the coat pocket, slipping the paper inside the lining, in an attempt to make them believe the message had never been missing. He had had ample opportunity, for he had been alone in the cabin that morning for some time while he made breakfast. The more Ronald thought about this possibility, the less he was inclined to disregard it.

Still another explanation presented itself, but one which did not appear as likely. The message might have been stolen by Jim Rivers. Ronald had not worn the coat that day, but had left it hanging in the cabin. Jim could easily have returned the message if he desired to do so. But what reason would Jim have to return the message if he had taken it? If he had stolen the message with the idea of preventing them from finding the mine, he would certainly not have done so. Perhaps he had seen Ted and Nelson make the discovery, decided the paper was important, and stolen it. He had been surprised to find the message was in code, and since it was useless to him, decided to return it. That might be an Indian's manner of reasoning.

This question, then, was still unanswered: Was the code message stolen, and if so, who took it, Mr. Gumber or Jim Rivers? If Mr. Gumber was telling the truth, there probably was an Indian on the mountain who might have stolen the message, or the explanation of its falling into the lining might be correct. But if he was not telling the truth, the Indian probably did not exist, and he had most certainly taken the message himself.

The trip down the mountain was a long one. The early darkness was due as much to the gathering of clouds as it was to the prospective setting of the sun. The wind was rising, thunder rolled in the distance, and jagged streaks of lightning played tag across the sky. They welcomed each brilliant flash, for then the trail showed more clearly before them. Neither of them felt much like talking, but occasionally when the silences grew too long one of them would make a remark.

"I guess the boys were pretty disappointed about not finding the mine," offered Mr. Gumber.

"Yes," said Ronald, "I suppose they were."

"It's pretty hard to feel that you're that close to something you want, and still not able to get it." He spoke with a conviction which surprised Ronald, and caused him to wonder.

"Everyone has disappointments, and a person just has to learn to accept them," said Ronald philosophically. "I suppose you have had some yourself."

"Yes," returned the engineer somewhat bitterly, "I guess I've had my share."

Ronald felt closer to Mr. Gumber than he ever had before, and wondered if after all his vague suspicions had been groundless. Yet he realized that he knew practically nothing about the man (who after all had volunteered little information about himself), and there were still the facts that he had appeared on the scene suddenly and at an unusual time, stating only briefly his reasons for his interest in the case. Again Ronald reproached himself for not having asked for the man's credentials at their first interview, but it seemed rather too late to go into that now.

The trip took them considerably longer than it would have under more favorable conditions, and it was quite dark by the time they reached the Breckridge farm. The farmer invited them in for a cup of coffee, but as the hour was growing late, they declined with thanks. He opened the barn door for them, and they drove out, thanking him again for his favor.

"I suppose you won't be in town very long," said Ronald as they drove back toward Forestdale.

"I don't know," said Mr. Gumber. "My plans are rather indefinite. I have some matters to attend to, and I don't know just how long it will take me."

"Then you'll be going home, I suppose," suggested Ronald.

"Home? I haven't had an established home for a long time. I've traveled about a good deal in recent years."

"But you must have had a home at one time," Ronald suggested again.

"Yes, I did once. I came from Pennsylvania originally, and took my engineering degree at the local college. Then I came west. But there's no reason why I should bother you with my troubles," and he broke off abruptly.

With a sudden thought, Ronald said, "You wouldn't have to return to the hotel. You're welcome to stay with us as long as you're in town. I know Mother won't mind. Ted won't be back, and you can have his room."

"Thanks," said the engineer, much touched by the offer, "thanks very much, but I don't think I'd better. I've intruded on your hospitality long enough, and I still have my room at the hotel."

So Ronald drove him back to the hotel. They shook hands and said good night. Mrs. Wilford noticed that Ronald remained very thoughtful the rest of the evening. He was turning over all the facts of the case, trying to make them fit together. Several new possibilities had been opened to him. For one thing, there was the scrap of paper he had found. He took it out and examined it carefully. If this was the paper Mr. Gumber had used to read the code message, as he had first supposed, was it possible to know what was on the burned portion of the paper?

Apparently each column had contained about a third of the letters of the alphabet. From the numbers given, it was logical to assume that all the numbers in the first column began with 1, in the second column with 2, and the third column with 3. The final figures in the groups seemed to follow in consecutive order, 1-2-3.

For the second figures, it would appear that, reading down the columns, there would be three 1's, followed by three 2's, and then three 3's. Ronald had now arrived at a table that looked like this:

A 111	J 211	S 311	B 112	K 212	T 312	C 113
L 213	U 313	D 121	M 221	V 321	E 122	N 222
W 322	F 123	O 223	X 323	G 131	P 231	Y 331
H 132	Q 232	Z 332	I 133	R 233	& 333	

And that was as far as he could go. He wished he knew of some code expert who could help him unravel the rest of the secret, but did not know exactly how to proceed without breaking the confidence the boys had given him.

Would it be wise to investigate the occupant of that other cabin, perhaps Jim Rivers? He did not really think it was Jim, for by this time he had about made up his mind that there never had been an Indian on the mountain. Whoever the occupant was, at least he could clear up the point about the Mother Goose book, and how little Tim entered into the case. But this was a step that could not be taken without taking the risk that they might disclose the secret of Old Goldie's cabin. Later, if the mine could not be found, and they were ready to abandon the search, it might be done.

One other thing Ronald was going to do was to try to check up on Mr. Gumber, for he felt certain that the engineer was concealing some important facts. It was strange that Ted should have thought Mr. Gumber looked familiar the first time they met. And then the feeling came to Ronald that he, too, should have recognized Mr. Gumber. At first it was only a vague thought, perhaps inspired by the remark Ted had made to him once on the subject, but the idea stayed with him and grew upon him.

The next morning the thought persisted, only by now it had taken more definite shape, and he determined to act upon it. He looked through his own file, but unable to find what he wanted he drove over to the office of the North Ridge *News-Record.*

"Remember that we were once discussing the firm Up-State Mining Enterprises which went bankrupt five years ago?" he said to Ken Kutler whom he found still at his office.

"Yes, I remember," said Ken, wonderingly.

"Would it be all right," said Ronald, "for me to check your file on that case?"

"Sure," said Ken, still wondering what Ronald was up to. He procured a folder from a drawer and handed it to Ronald. Ronald took it, and carefully looked through the clippings, while Ken watched him closely.

"Your paper covered that story pretty thoroughly," said Ronald. "You even have pictures of the three partners."

"Yes," said Ken, "the case was of widespread interest because of the way Old Goldie's mine entered into it, and because a lot of people around here lost money in the company."

Ronald closed the folder and handed it back to Ken, who was wondering desperately what Ronald was checking up on, and whether he had found what he wanted. Ronald thanked him, and left him still guessing. As he drove back to Forestdale, Ronald had to smile at the manner in which he had managed to keep Ken confused, but the smile soon faded and a more serious look took its place. The discovery he had just made changed the entire aspect of the case, and he wondered how it would fit in with the other facts. For now he knew that the man who called himself Mr. Gumber was really Frederick Fairchild, the junior partner of Up-State Mining Enterprises.

CHAPTER 19

Trapped

The cabin seemed lonely after the others left. With the fall of night the rain came back in earnest. For a time the storm raged, and then settled down into a steady downpour.

"I hope they didn't get caught in the storm," said Nelson after a long silence.

"I don't think they did," said Ted. "They should have been back in town before this."

Nelson voiced the thought that was in both their minds. "It's queer how Ron found the code message in his pocket.

I'm glad he did, though. I didn't really believe Mr. Gumber took it. He's a nice sort of fellow."

"Yes, I think so, too," agreed Ted. Ronald had not voiced to them his doubts about the hole in his pocket, so naturally they accepted his explanation at full value. Nor did it occur to them that the scrap of paper Ronald had found in the fire was of any importance. They had thought that Mr. Gumber had been trying to break the code message he had stolen, but now that they no longer suspected him, they had no doubt that there was some other explanation for the paper he had tried to burn.

The evening would have seemed tiresome had it not been for the hopes they still held—although dimmer than before—finding the mine, and the apprehension they felt concerning a possible return of the Indian Mr. Gumber had seen at the window. It was all right to joke about the Indian in the daylight, but alone in the cabin at night the situation was a lot different, and many times they caught themselves glancing up at the window, almost expecting to see a bronzed face peering in at them.

To keep their thoughts occupied, they talked about the case, and especially about their plans for carrying on the search. They both felt that the territory already covered had been rather thoroughly explored. Their best chance, then, was to enlarge the circle about them.

"We could start up the mountain like we did today," suggested Nelson, "and search just beyond the part we covered today, going in a big circle all the way around." This plan was agreeable to Ted. Neither of them felt much like going to bed, but the evening dragged on, and finally they undressed and climbed into the bunk, sleeping more soundly than they expected.

By morning the rain had stopped, but the weather had not cleared, and they could look forward to more showers throughout the day. The ground was wet, and it was therefore an unpleasant day for their search, but they did not let this stop them. After an early breakfast they set out up the mountainside, and proceeded to carry out the same careful search they had made the day before.

Walking was difficult, for the mud accumulated on their hiking shoes, making their feet feel heavy, and the trails were slippery in many places. They each fell several times, but after they made sure no injuries were sustained, each mishap became a reason for a laugh. Indeed they did present a ludicrous appearance, splattered by mud.

By eleven o'clock the sun had come out, and they picked out a sunny spot on a rock overlooking the spring to stop for lunch.

"I wonder if we're going to find that gold mine after all," said Nelson, idly tossing a pebble into the water and watching the ripples spread out to shore.

"Everything would be easy if we could only read that code message," said Ted, leaning on his elbow, looking upward at his friend.

"Maybe we could read it, if we worked at it hard enough," said Nelson. Lying back, he decided that even if he had a million dollars he would never enjoy anything more than lying there and watching the clouds drift lazily across the sky.

"I don't think so," returned Ted. "The only person who can read that code message is T.A.F., and if he ever gets hold of the message, our chance of finding the mine first will be gone."

For ten minutes they continued to enjoy their brief period of complete relaxation. That is, Nelson was completely relaxed, but Ted's thoughts were active.

"Somehow I can't help but feel that we should be able to find that mine," he said. "All the pieces are here if we only knew how to put them together." He lay quietly for a few minutes, and then announced in a soft, almost dreamy, voice, "I think I know where that mine might be."

Nelson sat up and stared at his friend, fearing for a moment that he had been affected by the sun. How could anyone discover a gold mine by lying down and looking up at the sky? Ted jumped to his feet and led the way back to the cabin. He spoke in a low voice, as though trying to keep his feeling of excitement well under control.

"Look, did it occur to you that this is rather an odd place to build a cabin?"

"No, it didn't," replied Nelson truthfully. "It did to me just now. The cabin is half a mile from the spring, so he could have built it closer to the water. If he wanted protection from the wind he should have set it closer to the cliff. Apparently the ground here had to be leveled and trees cleared away. There must have been better locations, so why build it here?"

"I thought we agreed he probably wanted to build it close to his mine," said Nelson.

"Exactly!" exclaimed Ted. "And in that case, why not build his cabin right over the mine!" Nelson started suddenly as though he had had an electric shock. It seemed incredible that the mine could be beneath the cabin, and yet why not?

"But how can we reach it if it is there? There's not enough room to crawl under the foundation."

"Perhaps there's a trap door in the floor," said Ted. "Let's look for it."

They dashed into the cabin, threw down the supplies they were carrying, and on hands and knees carefully explored every inch of the floor. The first time they found nothing, but going over it again Nelson discovered a small knot hole through the floor under the table. By placing his finger through the hole he was able to lift a section of the floor a little more than a foot square. His exclamation brought Ted to his side, and together they peered down into the black depths.

At first they could see nothing, but the beam of the flashlight revealed a narrow shaft going straight down for about twenty feet. An old rope ladder, suspended from two rusty nails, served as a means of descent. The trap door itself was attached by leather hinges on the under side which prevented the door from being laid entirely back. So evenly had it been matched into the pattern of the floor that it is unlikely it would have been noticed unless someone suspected that it was there.

"Let's go down!" cried the adventuresome Nelson.

"Are you sure the ladder will hold us?" asked Ted, a little more cautiously.

Nelson hauled up the rope ladder and tested its rungs.

"It'll hold an elephant. Come on!"

Suiting his actions to his words, Nelson grabbed the flashlight and began the descent, soon standing at the bottom of the shaft and calling impatiently for his companion to follow. Ted was lighter than Nelson, who was inclined to be overweight, so it is not easy to understand what followed. Apparently the rope hanging on one of the nails had slipped farther toward the head of the nail, thus creating added pressure downward.

Ted had barely begun the descent when the nail bent slightly. There was a splintering of the wood, which must have been weakened by exposure and dampness, and the nail gave way altogether. The sudden doubling of weight on the other nail also caused it to bend, and the rope ladder fell off entirely, dropping Ted to the bottom of the shaft with a suppressed cry.

Had the ladder fallen from both nails at the same instant he might have escaped injury, but because one nail gave way first he dropped at an angle, and his ankle crumbled beneath him. He lay where he fell, stunned, unable to rise to his feet.

"Ted, are you hurt?" cried Nelson in alarm. Ted strove to recover his whirling senses.

"I guess—I hurt my ankle a little," he said, struggling to make his voice sound steady, and to suppress the tears which threatened to break through to the surface in spite of all he could do to force them back. Gradually the seriousness of their predicament dawned upon them. The trap door had swung shut over their heads, and they were buried in the heart of the mountain.

"Do you think anyone will be able to find us?" asked Nelson in a hushed whisper.

"Ron said he might come back in a few days," said Ted, speaking through clenched teeth. This, then, was their only chance of outside rescue—a promise by Ronald that he might come back.

"Even then, will he be able to find us?" asked Nelson gloomily. "We can shout, but I don't think he could hear us. The wind is rising again, and the storm is coming back."

"We'll have to make him hear us," said Ted desperately. But he knew that the coming storm was an important factor, for it might cause Ronald to postpone his return to the mountain. By such small things is the destiny of a person sometimes decided. For if Ronald knew they were in trouble, he would have overcome almost any obstacle to reach them.

Ted remembered how Mr. Gumber had been trapped in a mine, but at least he had known someone was trying to reach him.

As a diversion Ted suggested that they explore the mine. A low tunnel led off from the shaft, and crawling through this they entered a large chamber about twenty feet square and seven feet high. It had the appearance of a natural cave, although in several places there was evidence of digging. Ted picked up several rocks and examined them closely. They were quartz, the only quartz they had seen in that vicinity. Both boys knew that gold was sometimes found among deposits of quartz. Was there a certain golden luster to the rocks?

But the flickering light was uncertain, and rather than arouse false hopes Ted resolved to say nothing. He had already made a discovery which he had previously suspected: that he was unable to stand unaided. An examination with the flashlight revealed that his ankle was bruised and discolored.

"Guess I'll have to rest it awhile," he said with an attempt at a laugh. There was a slight dampness in the cave, and as it began to penetrate through them they were glad to sit close together, preparing to while away the long hours ahead—how many they did not know. They talked about the mine, and how glad Ronald would be to get his story, but avoided all reference to their present predicament or the chances of rescue. Before long the conversation began to lag, and finally dwindled away altogether. Perhaps they fell asleep.

CHAPTER 20

An Explanation

Upon his return to Forestdale, Ronald went directly to the hotel and asked at the desk for Mr. Gumber. The clerk put through a call, then told Ronald Mr. Gumber would see him upstairs. The engineer greeted him cordially, although somewhat puzzled by the unexpected call and Ronald's seriousness of manner. Ronald came directly to the point.

"I believe I am correct in addressing you as Mr. Fairchild?" The engineer was startled by the sudden charge.

He turned his eyes away, and admitted slowly, "Yes, my name is Fairchild."

"You are Frederick Fairchild, junior partner of Up-State Mining Enterprises?" persisted Ronald.

"Yes, I am Frederick Fairchild," the engineer admitted again. As Ronald made no attempt to continue, he said, "I know what you must be thinking of me."

"I'm afraid I don't know quite what to think," returned Ronald, somewhat sternly.

"Perhaps you would care to hear my explanation," said the engineer in a humble manner.

"I'm prepared to listen to anything you have to say," said Ronald, not very graciously, accepting the chair the engineer offered him.

"Then I shall begin with the period immediately following my graduation from engineering school. I came to this state, and before long secured a position with Up-State Mining Enterprises in North Ridge.

"This firm was owned by two partners, Mr. Reegan and Mr. Jamison. They were eager to break in a young man with the idea of eventually raising him into a partnership. They treated me very well, although sometimes I suspected that they did not know as much about mining as they pretended. The salary they paid me was really more than an inexperienced engineer just out of college could have expected, although to do myself justice I did work very hard. On one of my first inspections for them I was caught in a cave-in, as I related to you the other night.

"For a time things went very well with me. I had married happily, and we had bought a home. I had a good job, and Mr. Reegan and Mr. Jamison were talking of taking me into the firm as a partner. I was very happy at the time, but I did not realize how short-lived my happiness was to be. The first blow came soon after. My wife died suddenly."

His voice was steady and unemotional, and he continued evenly: "About two years later I was made a partner in the firm, after making an investment of several thousand dollars. I was still young, and it was pleasing to my ego to be considered a partner rather than an employee, and to have my name on the door and on the stationery. I expected that my share of the profits would be considerably more than my old salary had been. It was about this time that my difficulties really began.

"It was a few months after I was made a partner that I began to be worried. It didn't take me long to discover that I was a partner in name only. I gradually became aware that the firm was having business dealings of which I knew nothing. For a time I did nothing about it, for I was unwilling to force the issue without definite proof. Then one day I secured evidence that some of the firm's money had been deposited in Mr. Jamison's personal account.

"I immediately confronted Mr. Jamison with the evidence, and demanded that as a partner all the company's records should be turned over to me for my inspection. He denied all my charges, making some plausible explanation, and for the time I thought that perhaps I had been mistaken. Mr. Jamison told me that he would have the records brought up-to-date that evening, and that I could examine them the following morning. I consented, and you can guess what happened. That night Mr. Reegan and Mr. Jamison cleared out, taking with them everything of value on which they could lay their hands.

"I had thought that the firm was operating on a profitable basis, but I soon discovered that the other partners had made several bad investments of which I knew nothing, and that the firm was heavily in debt. As a partner, I was, of course, liable for all the debts of the firm. My investment in the company was gone, my home foreclosed, my bank account attached, even my insurance policies liquidated and the money turned over to the creditors. Everything I possessed was taken from me, except for the small allowance which the law allows debtors in such instances.

"As if this were not bad enough, I was indicted on criminal charges. It was no surprise to me that I was found guilty, for I had indeed been guilty of negligence. The law presumes that partners should be familiar with the affairs of the firm, and I could see that I had made a blunder in not insisting from the beginning that no transactions should be carried on without my approval. Yet I had trusted Mr. Reegan and Mr. Jamison, and had thought that as time went on they would acquaint me more fully with affairs. The reason they did not do so I attributed to the fact that I was very busy during my first few months as a partner.

"In view of the fact that I had been innocent of criminal intentions, I received only a suspended sentence. But the creditors had lost thousands of dollars. Some of these people were personal friends of mine, and I resolved to pay the company's debts in full if I ever could.

"But this, it seemed, I would never be able to do, for something far more valuable than my property had been taken from me. My reputation was gone, and I found it impossible to secure another position in my profession.

"For the next five years I wandered about the state, picking up what jobs I could. There were many engineering positions I could have had, but as soon as employers learned of my background they decided to make other arrangements. I thought of going away and changing my name, but in that case I would have been no better off, for I would have been unable to produce my college diploma or to give any references.

"Those years were no particular hardship for me, for when I chose engineering as a profession I had not expected that things would always come my way. I had anticipated that I would occasionally have to rough it, to meet and overcome obstacles. I had many interesting experiences, and I believe I would really have enjoyed those years had it not been for the cloud which was hanging over me.

"Affairs continued in this manner up until a few months ago. I admit that by this time I was growing desperate. A situation had arisen whereby I simply had to have a large sum of money soon, and I was getting to the point where I hardly cared how I got it. This will be hard for you to understand, unless at some time you have needed money so badly that your sense of values was disturbed. I suppose that after enough people come to look upon you as a thief you eventually reach the point where you no longer care whether or not you are a thief.

"Then I heard about Old Goldie's death, and the stampede to the hills which had been caused by your newspaper stories. It occurred to me that possibly I could raise the money I needed by finding that mine. No other course seemed open to me, for it was impossible for me either to earn or to borrow the sum I needed. I searched the hills for weeks, but I did not know about the photograph's being reversed, and like everyone else I was searching on the wrong side of the mountain.

"When the mine could not be found, I decided to have an interview with you, for I thought you might have some additional facts you had not published which would be of help in finding the mine. Here I did my first dishonorable act. I knew that if I introduced myself as Mr. Fairchild you might recognize the name and refuse to talk with me, believing me to be a thief as everyone else did. So I registered at the hotel as Mr. Gumber— a rather unusual name; coming from my mother's family. I told you some of the facts about myself, which were true enough as far as they went, and you appeared to accept me in good faith.

"My interview with you was not a success, for apparently you had no other facts which would be helpful. But as we were leaving the hotel I had my first break. Ted met us at the door with his tale of having found Old Goldie's cabin.

"When Ted told how the photograph had been reversed, I knew that now I would be able to find the cabin myself. Still, it might be that other facts would be discovered which would help indicate the location of the mine, so I requested that I be made a member of the party. If this seems an infringement upon hospitality, remember that I was almost frantic under the pressure of raising a large sum of money in the near future. I might add that I wanted very much to confess at this point, and request that I be taken in as a member of the party on equal shares if the mine was discovered, since it was possible that my engineering training might be of help in locating it, or I would have been satisfied merely to be placed in charge of mining operations if the money I needed would be advanced to me. But I could not bring myself to confess, for the fact that I already had used a false name would have made you doubly suspicious. Thus I had already woven a web from which it was difficult to untangle myself.

"I went up to the cabin with you, but the search we made convinced me that the mine was not going to be easy to find. Since I now knew all the facts the rest of you knew, there was no point in my remaining there any longer, and your leaving that evening gave me a chance to come back with you. After the boys became discouraged and gave up the search, then I would return to the mountain again."

As the engineer finished speaking, Ronald leaned forward, his manner somewhat softened by the tale, "Would you mind telling me one more thing, Mr. Fairchild? Was the reason you were so eager to find the mine due to the fact that you wanted to raise the money to repay the creditors of Up-State Mining Enterprises?"

"I could deceive you by saying so," said Mr. Fairchild, "and the possibility of repaying the creditors has always been in my mind. But no, that was not my principal reason for wanting to find the mine. The money I needed was for something much more personal, a matter I would prefer not to discuss."

"Then that is all you have to tell me?"

"Yes, that is all I can tell you now," he returned. Ronald rose to leave.

"I'm sorry, Mr. Fairchild. You certainly haven't had an easy time of things. I wish we could have met under different circumstances, for I think you are the kind of person I would have liked for a friend. But you can understand my position in these circumstances. You introduced your self to me giving a false name and under false pretenses. I was responsible for making you a part of our expedition when your only object was to use the information the boys had gathered for your own purpose."

He turned and left the room without attempting to shake hands. But Ronald was a fair-minded person, and his conscience troubled him the rest of the day. Mr. Fairchild certainly had run through a long streak of bad luck, and he could not be certain that if he were in Mr. Fairchild's place he would not have done the same thing. Acting on an impulse he returned to the hotel late in the afternoon.

"I'm sorry," said the clerk, "but Mr. Gumber has checked out."

CHAPTER 21

A Strange Rescue

For Ted and Nelson in their prison within the earth the hours dragged on endlessly. Occasionally they dozed off, for they were more exhausted than they realized, but for the most part Ted was too conscious of his throbbing ankle to be able to drift into sleep. Nelson was inclined to blame himself for their misfortune.

"I was too anxious to explore the mine, and I didn't think to test the nails as well as the ladder."

"Nonsense," said Ted, "it was my fault just as much as yours."

"There must be a way for us to get out," said Nelson desperately. "I wonder what Old Goldie would have done if he had been trapped in here."

"There may have been another entrance then," replied Ted. "Notice how the cave seems to lead away toward the surface. That was probably the entrance to the cave. Old Goldie filled it in with rocks after digging the shaft and building his cabin over it.

"If that was the real entrance, maybe we can get out by digging," suggested Nelson. They did try to dig a little, but it was an almost impossible task with only their hands and Nelson's jackknife for tools.

"I don't think it's any use," said Ted at last. "This wall seems to be just as solid as the rest of them."

Nelson crawled back through the tunnel to explore the possibility of escape up the shaft. It was too wide to permit a person to climb it by bracing himself between opposite walls. The only alternative was to cut footholds in the side. He made a start at this, but the stony and sandy characteristic of the soil made this method unpromising.

Realizing it was futile, he nevertheless worked at it intermittently, for it gave him something to do. Persons with time on their hands usually become hungry, and as the afternoon wore on the boys became increasingly conscious of the emptiness within their stomachs. Theirs had been but a light lunch, and it was a long time since breakfast; indeed they had not had a heavy meal for three days.

"What I could do to a crisp steak smothered in onions," said Nelson, breaking a long interval of silence.

"Or lamb stew with scalloped potatoes," sighed Ted. Just now he could think of nothing more enticing than a warm meal and a comfortable bed. But he would have been satisfied if only the pain in his right ankle would let up just a little.

Their imprisonment was extremely unpleasant, for in addition to the dampness they were forced to sit in darkness most of the time. The flashlight was dimming, and the batteries could not last much longer. As time passed there was a growing apprehension within themselves that they were going to be imprisoned for a long time—that, indeed, they might not be found at all. But this was a thought which it was unwise to dwell upon, and they hastened to divert their thoughts into more pleasant channels.

"Anyway, we found Old Goldie's mine," said Nelson. "Half the people in the county were looking for it, but we were the ones to find it."

"You might say I fell into it," said Ted, trying to be humorous, which was difficult under the circumstances. Nelson looked about him.

"If this is Old Goldie's mine, shouldn't there be some tools or machinery around?"

"He must have taken his tools away with him. It looks like the place has been deserted for the last two years, as those old newspapers showed. That may be why the wood became rotten and the nails gave."

"I wonder if this mine really is worth a million dollars," said Nelson speculatively.

"It might be worth nothing at all. Perhaps it's all worked out, and that's why Old Goldie didn't come here for two years."

Ted was not naturally pessimistic, but he thought it wise to curb Nelson's dreams before his air castles came tumbling to the ground.

"But it must be valuable or Old Goldie wouldn't have gone to so much trouble to hide it, and leave the photograph and the code message. And he never worked it much himself, for he never seemed to have much money."

Although not ordinarily imaginative, Nelson could not surrender his visions of great wealth—if they were ever to have the opportunity of enjoying it.

"I wonder how long we've been down here," said Ted at last. In his fall his wristwatch had received a hard knock, breaking the crystal, and he had been unable to start it again. "It must be getting on toward evening."

Nelson crawled to the foot of the shaft and shouted, but he knew his voice would be lost among the gusts of wind which came faintly to their ears—even if there had been anyone to hear. He had another idea, that perhaps by tossing rocks up against the trap door he might be able to throw it open again making their discovery more certain should anyone enter the cabin, but either the trap door was too tightly fitted in place or else the task was beyond his skill, and he gave up at last.

Discouraged, he crawled back into the large chamber. There was nothing they could do but wait. They had lost all track of time. The conversation died out, and Nelson must have fallen soundly asleep, while even Ted, exhausted from the strain of the recent school year, their subsequent search for the mine, and their present ordeal, fell into a light slumber.

How long he slept he did not know. Had he been asked he would probably have guessed that it was well past midnight, although actually it was not yet eight o'clock. A slight sound aroused him, and in an instant he was wide awake.

"Nelson," he called, "there's someone in the cabin!" Nelson was instantly awake. They listened, and they could hear faintly the sound of footsteps on the cabin floor. Nelson crawled through the tunnel, Ted following, and stood at the bottom of the shaft, shouting with the full power of his lungs. The trap door opened, and a beam of light fell across the bottom of the shaft.

"'Ullo," came the voice from above, which they immediately realized did not belong to Ronald, as they had half expected.

"Hello, up there!" Nelson shouted back. "We're trapped down here. Let down a rope."

The trap door, which apparently would not stay open by itself, was closed again, and they guessed that the man above was looking about the cabin for a rope. Presently the door opened again.

"No rope here."

"Tell him to let down a string," said Ted, who was still crouched in the tunnel and could not make himself heard distinctly from above.

"A string!" echoed Nelson. "Do you think we can climb up a string like a monkey?"

The prospect of immediate rescue had restored his sense of humor.

"Tell him," urged Ted, and Nelson did so. The boys had wrapped their blankets and other bundles with heavy twine, so it was no problem for the man above to assemble a line which was soon dangling down the shaft. Nelson marveled at his own slow thinking as he saw Ted tie the string to the fallen rope ladder, which was then hoisted up. There was the sound of pounding as a new fastening was made, and soon the ladder was suspended securely from the floor above.

Ted could stand only with difficulty, but Nelson, standing behind him, grasped him about the chest with one arm, and in this fashion they ascended the ladder together. Several times it swayed precariously and they were in danger of losing their balance, but each time equilibrium was restored and the climb continued. As they neared the top their rescuer reached down and lifted Ted through the opening, and Nelson scrambled up after. He turned to thank the man, and a gasp of surprise escaped his lips.

The man was dressed in rough clothes, as would be expected of a person engaged in outdoor activities. His hair was combed back in an ordinary fashion, but was raven black, and his facial characteristics and the tint of his skin showed unmistakably that their benefactor was an Indian! The red man wasted no time for words, but helped Ted to a chair before the fireplace. By the light of the flashlight he gently removed the shoe and sock and felt the injured limb with skillful fingers.

"Hm, ankle broke," said the Indian.

"I know," returned Ted simply. Nelson looked at Ted in surprise. It had not occurred to him that Ted's injury was more than a sprain, for in the long hours they had spent underground Ted had hardly referred to it. He had long admired his friend, but a display of courage of this kind was something new to him. He knew that there are several different kinds of courage: mental courage, the willingness to support and fight for one's opinions; moral courage, the readiness to do what one believes is right; and outright physical courage. That Ted possessed the first two of these types he had long been certain, and now Ted had just displayed the third in its highest form.

"Need strips of cloth," said the Indian. As nothing better presented itself, Ted removed his shirt, and the Indian tore it into strips, binding them about the swollen member. With the ankle securely bound, he stood up and looked about him. The fire had been extinguished that morning and had not been rekindled. It was the work of a few minutes to build a fire, and a welcome blaze sprang up, warming the air. The boys had not been aware until then that their teeth were chattering.

Realizing that they must be hungry, the Indian looked through their supplies. He selected two cans of beans, opened them, and warmed them over the fire, also putting on water to which he later added chocolate. Strips of bacon and slices of potatoes were placed in the frying pan and done to a nice crisp.

They tore into their meal as soon as it was ready, refilling their plates several times. Everything tasted just right, but in their condition it is likely that even if the beans were cold and the bacon burned they would have tasted almost as good. The Indian stood watching them, smiling, refusing their invitation to take part in the repast. They wanted to question him, to ask him how he knew about the mine and that they were trapped in it, but did not feel that they could. Finally, as with his work finished the Indian looked about and seemed to be ready to make his departure, Nelson's curiosity could be restrained no longer.

"Are you Jim Rivers?" he demanded. The Indian's reticence was not to be broken in this fashion.

"You know Jim Rivers?" he replied, and with a wave of farewell he left the cabin and disappeared among the storm-swept trees.

CHAPTER 22

A Meeting

Gratified though they were at their unexplained rescue, the boys realized that their problems were by no means over. The bandage the Indian had put on Ted's foot was only a sort of first-aid sling, and the ankle still required proper medical attention. But how were they to get Ted down the mountain if he could not walk?

The mine, too, was a problem. They should, they supposed, be staking out a claim and getting it filed the next morning, but they didn't have the slightest idea how to go about it. And the property should be guarded, too. But maybe all this didn't matter, for Jim Rivers must have known where the mine was all the time, and maybe he had his claim filed already.

If only Ronald would come, he could relieve them of all these worries, and they could go to sleep. And Ronald did come, but this was several hours later, at close to twelve o'clock, when they thought it must be almost morning. He startled them when he pushed open the door and stood there, the water pouring off his coat. But more surprising was that Doctor Pearson was just behind him. They took off their wet hats and coats.

"That's the very first time in my life I've climbed a mountain at night during a storm," said Doctor Pearson. "I haven't had so much fun since I was a boy. Now we'll see about that ankle, young man."

Ted sat down before the fire, and the doctor removed the bandage.

"But what are you doing here?" asked Ted.

"I don't know what we're doing here," replied Ronald, with a worried look on his face. He watched the physician carefully force the bones back into place. During the ordeal Ted's teeth were set, and no sound escaped his tightly closed lips. As the physician finished his work, Ronald paced up and down.

"I received an anonymous telephone call," he explained at last, "saying that your ankle had been injured. I immediately got in touch with Doctor Pearson, and he thought we should come up at once."

"A telephone call!" exclaimed Ted. "Was it Jim Rivers?"

"No, I don't think it was Jim," said Ronald. "As I remember Jim spoke rather poor English, but this man sounded well educated. He kept his voice low, as though he was trying to disguise it, and hung up before I could ask any questions."

"Then it was someone you know," Ted pointed out, and Ronald smiled at the quick way in which Ted had figured that out.

"But what made you think of Jim Rivers just now?" asked Ronald.

"Because he was here in the cabin!" replied Ted.

"We would have been in a mighty tough spot without him," put in Nelson. So Jim Rivers had been in the cabin! Ronald, having about made up his mind that the presence of an Indian on the mountain was only a hoax, found it hard to readjust his ideas.

"I don't understand," he said. "How did the accident happen?"

"I fell down the mine shaft," replied Ted. He spoke casually, thinking that since Ronald already knew of the accident he must also know of the discovery of the mine.

"The mine!" exclaimed Ronald. "Where is the mine?"

"Right here under the cabin!" said Ted.

"We slept right over it for three nights," added Nelson. Quickly the story of their discovery and rescue was told. It would have been difficult under the circumstances to keep the story of the mine from Doctor Pearson, and the boys made no such attempt. But the doctor caught a questioning glance from Nelson, and said, "You don't need to worry about me, son. I know secrets about every family in town, and I guess I can keep one more."

"Anyway everyone in town will know about the mine in a day or two," said Ted. Ronald rose from his chair and paced about again.

"This affair is becoming very strange. You aren't sure the Indian was Jim Rivers?"

"No," said Ted, "but he must have been." Nelson thought so, too.

"But then he must have known where the mine was all along," said Ronald, "and could certainly have filed a claim to it by this time."

"Unless he was spying on us," suggested Nelson, "and saw us discover the mine."

"That would be possible," admitted Ronald, "but it still doesn't explain the telephone call I received. I'm quite certain that wasn't Jim."

There were a good many other unexplained features of the case, too, starting from the very beginning with the reversed photograph and the initials T.A.F. Ronald thought it best to acquaint the boys with the discoveries he had made regarding the mining engineer, and they listened in silence while he told the story.

"Jiminy, it was a good thing we didn't discover the mine while he was with us," said Nelson. "He might have filed a claim first, or found some other way of cheating us out of it."

Ted sat quietly for a moment, then said, "I feel sorry for him. It must be pretty bad to find yourself forced out of your profession because of something you couldn't help. I—I almost wish he had found the mine ahead of us."

Nelson's sympathy did not extend to such a length, but he found that he, too, was not feeling as elated over their discovery as he had before. No matter what the mine was worth, it would probably be at least enough to see them through college, perhaps pay the mortgage on his home, and provide for countless other things he wanted to do—but still, the mine would have meant so much more for Mr. Fairchild. He could have cleared his reputation by paying off the old creditors of Up-State Mining Enterprises, and established himself in his profession again.

Ronald, too, was rather quiet in view of the fact that he had just uncovered the biggest story of his career. He had already decided on one course of action—that he would investigate the occupant of that other cabin at Moosehead Pass. But there was a more immediate problem. It was necessary that they should file a claim to the mine as soon as possible, but he was at a loss as to how to proceed. His knowledge of mining operations was limited, and unless the claim was carefully staked out most of its value might be lost to them.

Their hike up the mountain had left Ronald and Doctor Pearson ready for another evening meal. More beans were opened, and coffee, which Ronald had included among the supplies he brought, was somehow brewed. Nelson and Ted also participated in the meal. The several hours' rest they had had before the arrival of the others had served to refresh them but Nelson was still a little unsteady on his feet, while Ted, of course, did not attempt to stand at all.

"I suppose we may as well try to get what sleep we can," Ronald suggested when they had finished.

"It hardly seems worth while," said Ted. "It'll be morning soon."

"Morning! It's hardly one o'clock." The two boys were surprised at the manner in which they had miscalculated the time. But before anything could be done there was an interruption. The door opened, and Mr. Fairchild stepped in out of the rain, looking about him uncertainly. Ronald stepped forward, extended his hand, helped the engineer off with his wet coat, and poured him a cup of coffee. The engineer drank part of the coffee, then looked around. From the silence which greeted him he must have realized that Ronald had told the others his story.

"It's all right," he said. "I know all about the mine."

"You do?" said Ronald. "Then you did steal the code message."

"Yes," returned the engineer, "I stole the message." He finished his coffee, then spoke slowly, "When Ted met us at the hotel with his story of the code message, I knew that that was the real clue to the location of the mine. That was my real reason for asking to become a part of your expedition—I wanted to get a copy of the code message.

"You may recall that although the code message was mentioned many times in my presence, no one ever produced it so that I might see it. I had only a brief glimpse of it when Ted handed it to Ronald in the hotel. If I had asked to see the message, it might have been turned over to me, but I was anxious to do nothing which might arouse suspicion. My only other course was to steal it.

"I had seen Ronald place the message rather carelessly in his coat pocket. I hoped to take the message, copy it, and return it. If it was missed in the meantime, Ronald might easily be made to believe he had lost it.

"I had no opportunity to take the message that first evening, so I decided that I would have to get up and take it during the night, for our plans were indefinite, and that might be our only night on the mountain. The plan was risky, for the sleeping arrangements were uncomfortable, and there was the chance that someone, especially Ronald, might be sleeping lightly. So I had a story all ready in case anyone should hear me.

"I knew that you had all heard of Jim Rivers, and were wondering if he knew about the mine. I knew also of Jim's presence on the mountain, and thought it likely that one of the boys might catch a glimpse of him while searching for the mine. The fact that Jim had been seen in town and that the smoke from the other cabin had been noticed were other points in favor of my plan. I resolved that if anyone should awaken while I was taking the message I would raise the cry of 'Indian!'

"At about one o'clock that night I thought that everyone was sleeping soundly. It was almost black within the cabin, for the fire had died out, and the clouds hid the moonlight. I arose quietly and made my way to the window. It was easy for me to obtain the message, but as I was returning to my bunk I had the misfortune to brush into a chair. Ronald started, and seemed about to awaken. I could take no further chances, and immediately cried out that I had seen an Indian at the window. You know the confusion that followed. I had one more piece of bad fortune, for the disappearance of the code message was immediately discovered.

"I thought that Ronald was rather doubtful about the explanation that an Indian had stolen the message. The next morning I was alone in the cabin for a few minutes. I hurriedly copied the message, made a small rip in Ronald's coat pocket, and stuffed the old copy into the lining, hoping he would think that it had been there all the time. Since I now had what I had come for, there was no more reason for me to stay on the mountain, and I left that evening when Ronald made his suggestion."

He looked about at the silent faces. "I am telling this badly. I should have started at the beginning. Since the mine has been found, there is no longer any reason why I should conceal anything from you."

So, with the two older men occupying the chairs, with Ronald standing by the fireplace, and with the boys sitting on the bunk, Mr. Fairchild began his tale.

CHAPTER 23

Old Goldie's Story

The engineer crossed his legs and settled back in his chair.

"To begin with, although I am known by the name of Frederick Fairchild, that is not my true name. My real name is Timothy Alfred Fairchild."

"T.A.F.!" murmured Ted under his breath. "But your name was given as Frederick Fairchild in all the old newspaper stories," said Ronald.

"Yes, but those circumstances were not of my doing. When I was in college there was another student whose name was Timothy Fairchild. There was some confusion of names, and for this reason I came to use my middle name. My diploma was made out to T. Alfred Fairchild, and so I decided to continue to use this name in business. To my more intimate acquaintances I was known as Fred, and many people came to believe that my name was Frederick. And so, in spite of the fact that my name was painted on the door those last few months, the indictment came to be made out against Frederick Fairchild. Later it was changed on the court records, but the newspapers continued to use the other name."

No one spoke, and after a pause the engineer continued, "To tell the whole story I shall have to go back more than forty years, some years before I was born. After leaving high school and before entering college, my father went west to a small mining town where there was a temporary boom on.

While there he made the acquaintance of a young man by the name of John Westlock, who was only a few years older than himself. The two took a strong liking to each other, and decided to team up together. So they became partners, and often went out on long prospecting journeys together.

"My father thought there was something queer about Westlock. He seldom spoke about himself, never wrote to his folks, and seemed to have no idea of ever returning to a settled home. He was a very quiet, reserved sort of person. He had few friends—in fact hardly anyone even knew his name—and he seemed to want to avoid people as much as possible.

"But over the camp fire in the long evenings the two young men often confided in each other, and at last my father was able to piece together his friend's story.

"John Westlock came from a wealthy family in Boston. His father, however, was very strict. He seemed unable to understand this quiet, dreaming boy of his, and would punish him severely for even the slightest offense. Like many other boys who are unduly suppressed at home, John became a little wild.

"When he was fourteen John became involved in some slight scrape. It was nothing serious as we would look at it nowadays, being only a thoughtless boyish escapade, but there was some property damage involved, and John was brought to court. The judge took rather a lenient view of the affair, and was willing to parole John in the custody of his parents, provided his father would make good the property damage.

"But this is the cruel part of the whole affair. John's father refused to pay for the damage, even though he could easily have afforded to do so. Then John pleaded for a chance to earn the money himself, but his father refused to accept the responsibility for his parole, and insisted that he should stand his full punishment under the law. So John was sent to a boys' reform school for two years.

"When he was released at the age of sixteen John saw no reason to remain at home—rather he was even ashamed to be seen on the streets of his neighborhood. His mother had died broken-hearted while he was still in reform school. He did not want to live with his father, and had no desire to inherit the estate which would some day have been his. So he ran away, going west, where he wandered about for several years before striking up an acquaintance with my father.

"On one of their prospecting trips one day, Westlock's horse shied at a rattlesnake in the path, throwing Westlock off and over a cliff. He was saved by being caught in a tree growing out of a small ledge on the face of the cliff, and my father, at the risk of his own life, climbed down after him, cut him free, and brought him back to the top. That cemented their friendship for life.

"Not long after that they made a small strike, and my father decided to take his share and return east to college. He tried to persuade Westlock to return with him, but Westlock was uninterested in the idea, and so they parted. That was the last time my father ever saw Westlock, although he had several letters from him later.

"As I grew up I decided that I wanted to be a mining engineer like my father. After my graduation, I came to this state, which my father suggested as a promising location, and it was while working for Up-State Mining Enterprises that I first met Old Goldie.

"He came into the office one day bearing a bag of gold ore. I found it to be richer than average, and naturally I was very curious about where he had gotten it, but he would answer no questions. So I purchased the ore from him and he went back to the mountains.

"This happened many times after that. Every few months, apparently whenever his funds ran out, he would bring in more ore to sell. Occasionally we would have time to talk together, and sometimes he would ask me questions, although he would never offer any information about himself. Once he learned my name he seemed to have a great deal of confidence in me, although at the time I could not understand why. Finally he refused to deal with anyone but me. If ever he happened to come in while I was not at the office he would leave and come back later.

"Then one day he told me that he was John Westlock, the prospector whose life my father had once saved. I was one of the few persons who ever knew his real name. He did not use it often, I believe, because it was the same as his father's. To everyone else he had become known as 'Goldie' because of the successful strikes he had made, and as the years passed the name became 'Old Goldie.' He seemed to prefer this nickname.

"Once I knew his real identity I did everything I could for him. I tried to persuade him to give up his manner of living alone, and even invited him to live with me. Failing in this I tried to do little things for him, such as inviting him to dinner, but he would never come. So far as I knew he was all alone, except for Jim Rivers, who sometimes accompanied him on his trips.

"At the time I thought that Old Goldie was still bitter, that he had allowed an incident in his boyhood to shadow his whole life. Now I believe that if he had once been bitter, the bitterness had long since left his heart. He enjoyed the free life of prospecting and living close to nature. Every tree and every bird was his friend, and most of them he could call by name. He knew the call of the whippoorwill, the smell of fresh, moist earth, the soft touch of a rabbit's fur, the crackling of fallen leaves, the force of the storm against his face, and he was happy.

"Being unsuccessful in getting him to change his habits, I urged that at least he should take out a legal claim to his mine and permit it to be worked by modern engineering methods, but this also he refused to do. I attributed this to a natural suspicion of the law and legal matters held by many poorly educated people. Later I realized that it might be due to something entirely different. He had lived in a wealthy home in his boyhood and he had not been happy, so he had no desire to be rich again. But he did want very much to be let alone. So he was satisfied to work his mine just enough to supply his needs for a few months ahead.

"Several years after this Old Goldie came into the office and told me that he wanted me to be the one to inherit his mine. He said that he had no living relatives, for he had been an only child. At first I did not see how this could be arranged, for he still refused to file a claim to the mine, and therefore he could not leave a legal will to it. He also seemed unwilling to give me the location of the mine, although I had already guessed that it was somewhere on Thunder Mountain.

"Then I hit upon an arrangement. I knew of a rather simple code, but one which it would be difficult for an outsider to break. I explained to him how the code worked, and he promised to leave me somewhere, written in code, a message giving the location of the mine. He said that the mine was well concealed, and that it was unlikely anyone would stumble upon it by accident. At the time I was only humoring the fellow, for I was well off financially, and did not care much if I ever owned the mine.

"It was not long after this that I became a partner in the company. I have already related to Ronald how the company went bankrupt, and I found myself suddenly deserted and responsible for the firm's debts. At my trial I learned for the first time that the other partners had induced many creditors to loan money to the firm by leading them to believe that the company owned Old Goldie's mine. But at the trial no one was able to produce any evidence to show that Old Goldie had sold his mine, and I knew that he had never done so.

"For five years I wandered about, picking up what jobs I could, until this spring when it suddenly became necessary for me to raise a large sum of money. It occurred to me that I might go to Old Goldie for the money I needed. I was not sure how he felt about me, for I had not seen him since my trial, and I thought that perhaps he might regard me as a thief just as everyone else did. Nevertheless I determined to try.

"But search as I would I was unable to locate him. He had not been seen for some time, and I thought it likely that he had taken the long prospecting trip farther west that he had once mentioned to me. I even enlisted the aid of Jim Rivers, who, I thought, would be able to find him if anyone could, but Jim was unable to help me.

"Then one day I heard of Old Goldie's sudden death at the North Ridge hospital, and believe me I was genuinely sorry to learn of it.

"There was still the necessity of raising the money I needed, and I knew that now I must find the mine myself. That night I sent a letter to Jim Rivers and he met me at the hotel. I explained to him that I wanted him to help me search for the mine, and he agreed. I was not familiar with the territory around Thunder Mountain, and thought that he would be of help to me as a guide. At this time, I did not actually register at the hotel, so there was no question later when I registered under an assumed name.

"By this time the papers were full of the story of Old Goldie's mine, and when I read the stories I knew he had not lost confidence in me. He had left the envelope for me, and I knew that the code message must be in the pine tree. He probably did not want to carry the code message with him for fear that it would have been printed in the papers, and might come into the hands of someone who would be able to break it.

"Jim and I spent weeks hunting for the cabin. We searched the western side, for I did not know then that the cabin was on the eastern slope. But now I can recall a conversation with Old Goldie in which we discussed photography, and I remember how he stressed the point that a picture would appear to be completely different if the negative was reversed. I did not know why he emphasized the point at the time, but he must have thought that I would recall the conversation and realize that the cabin was on the eastern slope. The photograph he deliberately reversed to make it more difficult for anyone to find the cabin ahead of me. It was a clever trick, but the trouble was that it fooled me as well as everyone else.

"Jim and I were unable to find the cabin. While staying at the cabin at Moosehead Pass, Jim returned one evening to find the two boys in the cabin. He followed them a short distance down the trail to determine if they were on their way home or were stopping on the mountain.

"About this time I determined to have an interview with Ronald. I went to the hotel and registered as Mr. Gumber, and requested Ronald to stop in. Later, learning about the discovery of the cabin and the code message, I invited myself along and stole the code message as I related. But was it stealing to take the message which had been meant for me, and which only I could read? And who had a better right to the mine than I did?

"The next morning, alone in the cabin, I replaced the code message in Ronald's pocket, and proceeded to read my own copy, later throwing my work in the fire. I now knew that the mine was under the cabin.

"You can imagine how tantalizing it was to know where the mine was and not to be able to go to it. It was important that I should do nothing in the least suspicious, for Ronald seemed doubtful about me, and kept me under close surveillance all day. Our searching that day was not completely useless, for my observations convinced me that there was no sign of gold anywhere else in the district, and that probably a gold deposit had been forced near the surface at one point by some freak of nature.

"We left the mountain that night, and the next day Ronald came to me with his accusations. I told him part of my story, which was all true, as far as it went. I might say that I was thoroughly ashamed of the way I treated the three of you, but I still needed that money, and I was determined to claim the mine if I could. I returned to the cabin at Moosehead Pass, and instructed Jim Rivers to keep an eye on the boys, so that I could know when they left. Jim came back with the report that the cabin appeared to be deserted, although all their things seemed to be there.

"What was I to do? They must have discovered the mine, and since they hadn't returned to the surface for a long time, there might have been an accident. If they were trapped I could not leave them down there, and yet I could not rescue them without giving myself away completely. I told Jim about the mine, and that he should go to the cabin and see if they were in trouble. He rescued the boys, and on his return told me about Ted's ankle.

"Knowing that such injuries can sometimes be serious if not properly taken care of, I went down the mountain and at a farm house put through a call to Ronald. Then I returned to the cabin, wondering what I should do. If I confessed would you believe me and let me earn the money I needed by putting me in charge of mining operations? I decided that that was the only thing I could do, so I came over here to tell you the story. That is the truth, and may a bolt of lightning strike me down if it's not."

Ted sat up suddenly. Where had he heard that expression before? No one spoke for a moment. Then Ronald went over to the engineer and extended his hand.

"I can't tell you how grateful I am, Mr. Fairchild. If it hadn't been for you the boys would still be down in the mine, and there is no telling what might have resulted.

Whatever decision is made belongs to the two boys, but for myself I want to say that I believe your story completely."

"Thank you for that," returned Mr. Fairchild, grasping the outstretched hand. Ted was not listening. He felt strangely hurried and excited. He know something— something Mr. Farichild had not included in his story— something he must tell the others. A lot of little things began to fit together: similarities in names and expressions, and a few casual remarks and incidents. For in a flash of intuition he suddenly realized why Mr. Fairchild had seemed familiar the first time they met, why he needed money so desperately, and the whole story of those initials.

CHAPTER 24

A Decision

As no one else spoke, Ted leaned forward and said quietly, "I think I know why you were so anxious to find the mine, Mr. Fairchild. You're Tim's father, and you wanted the money for an operation this summer."

Mr. Fairchild rose and walked over to the window. "Yes, I'm Tim's father," he said. He paused, then spoke again without turning around.

"My wife was involved in an accident just before Tim's birth. She died when he was born, and Tim was crippled. I hadn't intended to give the child my own name, but when I knew he was to be crippled, I did—like the Tiny Tim of Dickens' story. Old Goldie became fond of Tim, and I think that was one reason he wanted me to have his mine. He gave Tim that Mother Goose book, which I understand you found in the cabin. Like you I thought there might be some clue in the book to the location of the mine, and that is why I took it there with me.

"I had been advised by doctors that an operation would have the best chance of succeeding if undertaken this year, and I was determined that Tim should have this chance no matter what I had to do to earn it for him. There is a surgeon in New York who has been having success with cases of this kind—but that would take a lot of money even beyond the surgeon's fee—traveling expenses, hospital bills, and private nurses for a long time afterward.

"I don't know how you found out about Tim. I wouldn't have told you about him if you hadn't guessed. My sister, Mrs. Stoneman, says that you were out there one day, but she refused to talk to you, thinking you meant to revive the old scandal about Up-State Mining Enterprises."

He turned back toward them. "Now you know the state of mind I was in, and why I did things I wouldn't ordinarily have done."

"Yes," said Ronald, "I think we understand."

To whom did the mine really belong? Ted and Nelson had discovered the mine, so it was theirs, and Mr. Fairchild would have been satisfied merely to have been placed in charge of operations. But they felt that they had a moral obligation to him, because of Tim, because Old Goldie had wanted him to have the mine, and because he had rescued them. They discussed the matter for an hour, each wanting to give more than he received, and finally an agreement was reached which left them all more than satisfied.

"Now we'll see about the mine," said Mr. Fairchild.

"At this time of night?" asked Ronald. "Can't it wait till morning?"

"It'll be just as dark down there in the morning," said Mr. Fairchild. He selected the most powerful of the flashlights and descended to the mine, Ronald following after him, while the others waited anxiously for his report.

"I'll bet it's worth a million dollars," exalted Nelson.

"It may be worth nothing at all," cautioned Ted. He did not really believe this, but felt obliged to offer this opinion to preserve the proper balance.

"I wonder why he is taking so long," said Nelson a few minutes later. "Maybe the mine is worthless and he hates to break the news to us."

"Oh, it must be worth something," argued Ted, and Doctor Pearson was forced to smile at the way the boys had completely reversed themselves.

* * * *

Forty-five minutes later Ronald and Mr. Fairchild returned to the surface, the latter wearing the first smile they had ever seen on his face. He looked about him at the expectant faces.

"It's a gold mine," he announced, as if there had ever been any doubt about it.

"Is it worth much?" asked Ted almost in a whisper.

"Well, it's hard to tell from the limited tests I was able to make," the engineer returned cautiously. "It certainly isn't a million dollar mine, as the rumors had it, but I'm quite certain we will find it profitable enough." Almost at the same time everyone breathed deeply, their last doubts removed. Then they laughed.

"There's one important decision you boys will have to make. If I were to make all the tests I would like, it will take several days, and there's always the chance someone will discover the secret. The other way to go about it, we can assume that Old Goldie knew his business, that this really is the main lode, and I can stake out a claim at once. Which will it be?"

Ted and Nelson looked at each other. "Let's assume Old Goldie found the main lode," Ted decided. Nelson agreed.

"With so many people on the mountain, we can't take any chances on a delay."

"There's one more thing," said Ted when the babble of voices had finally faded, "could you tell us how that code works?"

"Certainly," said Mr. Fairchild. "To use the code you have to have a certain table." From his pocket Ronald drew out his notebook, and opened to the page on which he had listed each letter of the alphabet followed by three figures.

"Like this one?" he asked, handing the notebook to Mr. Fairchild. It was the engineer's turn to be amazed.

"Where did you get this?" he asked.

"When you threw your papers into the fire one of them wasn't entirely burned. From the piece I found I was able to build the whole table."

"Well, I guess I wasn't as clever as I thought," said Mr. Fairchild. "Your table is exactly right." He took up his explanation. "Old Goldie wanted to write the message, TRAP DOOR IN FLOOR OF CABIN. To do this he found each letter on the table, and wrote the proper three figures below each letter of the message."

On a paper he wrote:

T	312
R	233
A	111
P	231
–	
D	121
O	223
O	223
R	233
–	
I	133
N	222
–	
F	123
L	213
O	223
O	223
R	233
–	
O	223
F	123
–	
C	113
A	111
B	112
I	133
N	222

"He then took the last figure in the message, which is 2, and placed it at the beginning. The numbers then looked like this."

He wrote:

2 312 233 111 231 121 223 223 233 133 222 123 213
223 223 233 223 123 113 111112 133 22

"Old Goldie wrote the figures once more, keeping them all in the same order, but regrouping so that there would be three figures in all the groups. The numbers then looked like this."

The next line on the paper read:

231 223 311 123 112 122 322 323 313 322 212 321 322
322 323 322 312 311 311 111 213 322

"Finally he used this same table once more. He found each group of numbers on the table and substituted the proper letter of the alphabet for each group—231 became P, 223 became O, and so on."

The final line on the paper read the same as the code message they had found: POSFB EWXUW KVWWX WTSSA LW.

"Boy, that's a peachy code," exclaimed Nelson.

"Is it hard to break?" asked Ted.

"It would be for an amateur," said Mr. Fairchild. "A code expert would be able to break it without much trouble. But there are ways in which it could be made more difficult, so that it would cause even a code expert a lot of trouble, particularly in a message as short as this one."

"Just what is the principle of this code?" asked Ronald. Doctor Pearson was also looking on, much interested, for the code was as new to him as it was to the others.

"The principle is that each letter of the message is changed into a series of numbers, the numbers are in some fashion revised or interchanged, and then they are changed back into letters again."

"I notice on this table," pursued Ronald, "there is the and-sign followed by the number 333. Is that important?"

"It might be at times," returned Mr. Fairchild. "When the numbers are interchanged, the number 333 might arise, in which case the and-sign would be substituted for it. That is because there are twenty-seven possible combinations of the three numbers, but only twenty-six letters of the alphabet."

So Old Goldie had after all used a code system which was too difficult for them, but he did not invent it himself, for it had been supplied by Mr. Fairchild. Ted and Nelson looked at each other, resolving that if at any time in the future it became necessary to send a secret message, they would use this code.

No one slept much during the remainder of that night. They had talked far into the early hours, and when finally they did roll themselves in blankets spread out upon the floor sleep would not come except in short spells. They were up early, and all their remaining provisions were assembled into an appetizing breakfast.

The cabin was a bustle of activity that morning. Mr. Fairchild's job was to stake out the claim, and he did this as carefully as possible, enlisting Ronald's help in writing a complete description of the property.

"You can come with me to the county court house to file the claim," said Mr. Fairchild to Ronald, in case there should still remain the slightest lingering suspicion in Ronald's mind.

"I don't think that will be necessary," returned Ronald. "I have other matters to attend to."

He was already planning his story, walking about the cabin and outside, taking notes and occasionally asking questions. With Nelson's camera he took pictures of the cabin and of all the members of the party, hoping they would turn out well in spite of the early hour.

"I don't think we should leave the property unguarded," said Mr. Fairchild.

"I'll stay," said Nelson eagerly.

"I think you've been through enough," said Doctor Pearson. "I'd much rather see you at home for a week, sleeping in your own bed and eating your mother's cooking."

This was enough inducement for Nelson.

"I would suggest that we get Jim Rivers over here," said Mr. Fairchild. "He would make an excellent guard, and we could count on him not to talk very much."

This was agreeable, so Nelson, who felt that he had fully recovered from the preceding day's misadventure, was dispatched on the errand. He returned alone about an hour later, saying that Jim Rivers would be along presently with all his equipment. The Indian did come, just as they were ready to leave, as uncommunicative as ever. The boys tried to thank him for the part he had played in their rescue, but he brushed their remarks aside with grunts.

Doctor Pearson assumed the task of superintending the means of getting Ted down the mountain. By suspending the blankets between two rude branches a litter was improvised. When Ted realized that he was expected to ride in this, he protested vigorously.

"I can walk all right if I can lean on someone's shoulder," he maintained.

"Young man," said Doctor Pearson sternly, "you are going to be carried down the mountain, so you may as well enjoy it." Shaking his finger at him, he added, "And next time you break your ankle, don't make me climb a mountain at midnight during a storm."

"How about that ankle, is it going to be all right?" asked Ronald anxiously, realizing how little the mine would mean if Ted's injury should be permanent.

"Oh, certainly. Six weeks from now he won't even know he hurt it."

"Six weeks!" exclaimed Ted blankly. "That's half the summer."

"If you're like most of my patients, by that time you'll be so proud of your crutches you won't want to get rid of them at all," but Ted disagreed with a vigorous shake of his head. So Ted, shirtless, and with only one shoe and sock on, was carried down the slope.

"At least I'm not the first person to lose his shirt over a gold mine," he said jokingly. The rain had stopped at last, and the trip was in the nature of a triumphal procession. Everyone enjoyed himself, and the joking and good-natured banter made the trip seem short. Most of the time two of them could manage the litter, but the others gave a hand where the footing was uncertain. Solicitous though he was of Ted's comfort, Ronald kept urging the party on.

"What's the hurry?" demanded Ted. "We've got all day."

"Maybe you have," returned Ronald, "but my deadline is twelve o'clock, and I've got a story to write!"

CHAPTER 25

At the Breckridge Farm

One morning in August two boys stepped from the bus in front of the Breckridge farm. Ted's crutches were a thing of the past, but he still favored his injured ankle. Mrs. Breckridge saw them out in front and came to meet them.

"We came for our bikes," explained Ted.

"My, but it's about time," said the farmer's wife.

"I hope they haven't been in the way," said Ted, "but we wanted to wait until I could ride again."

"Of course they haven't been in the way, but I've been reading about the mine in the paper, and I've been bursting with questions I wanted to ask you. Now sit right down and get ready to tell me all about it." She went into the house and reappeared a little later with a tray holding two glasses of milk and a plate of cookies. So they munched cookies and talked willingly, for there was no longer the slightest need for secrecy.

"I understand your brother Ronald has left Forestdale," she began. "I suppose he has plenty of money now with his share of the mine."

"Oh, no," said Ted quickly, "Ron refused to accept a share in the mine. He said it was just a newspaper story to him." He added with pride, "But he got out of it what he wanted most after all. Mr. Fairchild gave him an introduction to an editor, and now he's gone to work on a city paper, just like he always wanted."

"I heard he just got out of town in time," said Nelson mischievously. "Everybody in town was hopping mad because he had them searching on the wrong side of the mountain. A lot of people think he reversed that photograph himself."

"Nothing of the sort," declared Ted shortly, feeling called upon to defend his brother's integrity. Ronald had been right about a good many things, but Ted knew that the mistake attributed to Ronald had been the cause of many humorous remarks about town. Maybe Ronald did get out of town just in time! Mrs. Breckridge broke up the friendly dispute.

"That's one thing I don't understand. Who really owns the mine, then?"

"We couldn't quite decide that either," said Ted frankly, "so we decided that the three of us would become equal partners, and the money Mr. Fairchild needed for Tim's operation we advanced him against his salary for running the mine for us. Of course we're going to pay back all the creditors of Up-State Mining Enterprises first."

"Well, that is good news," exclaimed Mrs. Breckridge, brightening up considerably. "Cy, did you hear that? We're going to get our money back from that mining company," and she went off in search of her husband.

"I wonder," said Nelson, as they relaxed on the lawn for a few minutes before starting the return trip, "as we think back about this years from now, what will we remember most?" The adventure had been full of thrills, but perhaps the outstanding one was that ghostly moment in Nelson's basement when they discovered that somehow, as though by magic, a picture of Old Goldie's cabin had appeared on Nelson's film.

"One thing I'll always remember," said Nelson, "is the way you sat down there in the mine all afternoon talking about rocks and things and never telling me your ankle was broken."

Ted looked off into the distance. To have earned such praise from Nelson was well worth two broken ankles, and a couple of broken arms thrown in.

"The thing I'll remember most," said Ted, "was the look in Mr. Fairchild's eyes when we told him we wanted him to share in the mine. That must have lifted a tremendous burden from his mind."

"Yes," agreed Nelson, "I'm glad we did the right thing by him." The right thing, thought Ted—how difficult it sometimes is to recognize it and to act upon it. If Old Goldie's father had done the right thing by him, the son's life might have been completely different. Yet in his own severe way the man had probably done what he thought was right.

There had been other thrilling moments in their adventure, too: Ted's sudden recollection of Tim's initials; the discovery of the Mother Goose book and the feeling of being followed; Mr. Fairchild's alarm in the night; the discovery of the mine, the awful emptiness of that moment when they realized they were trapped, and the strangeness of their rescue; and not least of all the thrill Ted had had that morning when a messenger boy handed him a telegram bearing the best news he had ever received:

OPERATION SUCCESSFUL. TIM WILL BE OUT OF HOSPITAL SOON. MR. FAIRCHILD RETURNING TO START MINING OPERATIONS. REGARDS. RONALD.

With many thanks to Mrs. Breckridge for the kindness she had shown, they mounted their bikes and headed back toward town. The road was a long down grade, and they coasted along at their leisure.

"Margaret Lake thinks you're pretty swell," shouted Nelson. "I heard her telling somebody how clever you were to discover where the mine was."

Ted tightened his lips, determined that he would not be teased.

"What do you say to baseball practice this afternoon?" asked Nelson as they entered the town. "Will you be able to play?"

"Oh, sure. Doctor Pearson says it's all right, so long as I don't do anything silly like sliding into bases."

"I'll call for you in a little while," Nelson promised, turning down his own street. When Ted arrived home he found the house empty. His mother had left a note promising to be home a little later, and advising him that there was a lunch waiting in the refrigerator if he was hungry.

Silently and alone he had his lunch. Never had the house seemed so big and lonely before. He left the kitchen and slowly climbed the stairs. How still everything seemed. The slanting rays of the afternoon sun cast a queer light through the hall, and contributed to the sense of loneliness.

He paused at Ronald's room, but all the personal effects had been removed. The bureau had been cleared off and the open clothes closet door revealed the emptiness within. With a slight shudder he passed on to his own room. For a moment he stood looking out the western window where sunlight sifted through stately elm trees and farther north Thunder Mountain stood silhouetted against the open sky.

He heard Nelson's whistle outside.

"Down in a minute," he called through the open window. Listlessly he changed into his baseball clothes. As he was about to leave the room he paused in front of the mirror, and as he stood there suddenly a new power surged through him. He had a feeling he had never had before, a control over obscure facial muscles he never knew were there. Deliberately he tightened up his face, and, yes, his ears moved back and forth, slowly at first, then more rapidly, but under perfect control.

"You're not a man until you can wiggle your ears," Ronald had said. A grin spread over his face. He grabbed up his glove, bounded down stairs, outside, and down toward the field.